P9-DIH-187
3 5674 05691699 3

Luciana

Out of This World

JUL 18

CH

JUL 18

☆ American Girl®

Luciana

Out of This World

BY ERIN TEAGAN

SCHOLASTIC INC.

Published by Scholastic Inc., *Publishers since 1920*. SCHOLASTIC and associated logos are trademarks and/or registered trademarks of Scholastic Inc. The publisher does not have any control over and does not assume any responsibility for author or third-party websites or their content.

This book is a work of fiction. Names, characters, places, and incidents are either the product of the author's imagination or are used fictitiously, and any resemblance to actual persons, living or dead, business establishments, events, or locales is entirely coincidental and not intended by American Girl or Scholastic.

Book design by Suzanne LaGasa
Author photo by Patty Schuchman
Cover and interior illustrations by Lucy Truman

Special thanks to Carmen Avila Silva, Chilean culture and Spanish language consultant at Commisceo Global Consultancy Ltd.

americangirl.com/service

ISBN 978-1-338-21272-3

10 9 8 7 6 5 4 3 2 1   18 19 20 21 22

Printed in the U.S.A.   23 • First printing 2018

FOR KAELYN, OLIVIA, KAIA,
AND ADDISON

CONTENTS

CHAPTER 1

A BIG TRIP

The plane landed hard on the runway and I jolted awake. With a rush I realized that we had just landed in my parents' home city: Santiago, Chile. My little sister, Isadora, dozed in her car seat next to me. I kissed her pudgy cheek in celebration.

"Wake up, Izzy!" I told her. "We're finally here!"

I live in Virginia with my parents and Izzy, but the rest of our family is in Santiago—cousins, aunts and uncles, great aunts, and Abuelita, my grandmother. Going back to Chile to see my family had been on my Christmas list ever since we visited six years ago, when I was in first grade. My wish finally came true this year when my parents told me that we would spend winter break in Santiago.

I turned to my mom across the aisle. "Who do you think will be at the airport to pick us up?" I asked. "I hope it's the whole family. With welcome signs and everything."

Mom looked at her watch. "It's pretty late, Luciana. It might just be Abuelita. Or maybe one of your uncles. But you'll see everyone soon enough."

I shook my head. I was certain my four favorite cousins would come to the airport to meet us. I had more than fifteen cousins in Santiago, and four of them— Julieta, Elena, Hugo, and Bastian—were twelve years old, just like me. I had messaged them our arrival time before we left, just to make sure that they would be there, but hadn't heard back yet. We used to message one another a lot, but lately—between becoming a big sister, school, and going to Space Camp and an astronaut training program—I'd been too busy to keep in touch. Now my only mission on this trip was to be with my family and catch up with my cousins. I had so many exciting things to tell them!

We stepped off the plane and then waited in line at customs, which seemed to take forever. As soon as we collected our suitcases at baggage claim, I grabbed Izzy's hand and we burst through the doors into the arrivals area. When I scanned the crowd, I saw lots of other families, and even a dog or two, waiting for their arriving travelers. But no one I recognized.

At last, by the back wall, I spotted a little white-haired woman wearing red reading glasses. My Abuelita.

"Luciana!" she called to me from across the room.

I scooped up Izzy and raced toward her, Mom and Dad struggling with the luggage behind us.

"*¡Mis niñas grandes!*" Abuelita said to Izzy and me. My big girls! She gave us a thousand kisses and pinches on our cheeks, and long, warm hugs. "*¿Cómo estuvo el viaje? ¿Comiste? ¿Estás cansada?*" Was it a good flight? Were we hungry? Tired?

I laughed. "*Está bien*, Abuelita," I reassured her.

Mom, Dad, Izzy, and I spoke Spanish a lot at home, but in Chile, where Spanish was the language, we'd speak it the entire time.

I squeezed Abuelita's hand. "Where is the rest of the family?" I asked her in Spanish. "I was hoping my cousins might be here."

"They cannot wait to see you," she replied. "But it is late and everyone is asleep by now."

I looked around. Most of the coffee stands and sandwich shops were closed up, but through the windows I could see that the city was bright with lights. I tried to hide my disappointment as I recalled the last time we came to Chile and found my cousins and aunts and uncles waiting for us as soon as we stepped into arrivals. They screamed and clapped, and ran to hug and kiss us. If my cousins came to Virginia, I'd greet them with balloons, even if it *was* three in the morning.

"You will see everyone tomorrow at the *asado*," Abuelita told me.

I perked up. "A barbecue? At your house?"

She nodded. "*Sí*."

I smiled. An asado at Abuelita's meant games, music, good food, and lots of fun.

I just had to be patient a little longer. Mission catch-up-with-my-cousins would start tomorrow.

CHAPTER 2

AN UNEXPECTED INVITATION

"Lulu! Luluuuuu! I up!" Izzy called to me from her crib. I rolled over on my air mattress and opened one eye to look at my sister. It was way too early to get up. Didn't I just go to sleep?

"Good morning," I said sleepily. Izzy stretched out her arms for me to pick her up.

I sat up and peered between the rails of the loft to the living room below. I heard the clinking of teacups and the soft thumping of cabinet doors coming from the kitchen downstairs. The big asado—it was happening today. Abuelita was up early so she could prepare the feast. I slid out of bed and walked over to Izzy's crib.

"Mama," Izzy said, pointing to a framed picture on the wall.

I peered at the photo. It was Mom and Dad on their wedding day. They had just moved to the United States so Mom could go to nursing school, and they looked so young and happy. I loved that picture.

I lifted Izzy out of her crib and showed her another one of my favorites—a photo of a black-haired baby in Abuelita's arms. "This is Mama too," I said. "When *she* was a baby."

All of the walls in the loft were lined with pictures in mismatched frames. There were so many pictures of holidays and birthday parties and graduations that I could barely tell the walls underneath were painted green. A twinge of a left-out kind of feeling fluttered in my heart because I was missing from so many of the family photos. But I hoped that by the end of my trip, there'd be at least one or two new photos of me and my cousins together up on that wall.

I pulled out my tablet to see if my cousins had replied to my last message, but there were no new messages. *They're probably still asleep,* I told myself.

When Izzy and I came downstairs, we found the big sliding doors to the patio open, the warm air blowing into the house. December meant winter back home in Virginia, but in Chile, it was the beginning of summer. My parents were helping Abuelita set up a table outside. Izzy scrambled out of my arms and ran past Mom and

Dad, straight for a big bouncy ball sitting against the back fence.

"*Buenos días, mi amor,*" Abuelita greeted me, chuckling at Izzy, who had rolled over the ball into the soft grass. "We'll have breakfast out here today. But first, can you fill this with more sugar?" she asked, holding out an empty crystal dish that had a crack down the side.

"Oh, it's broken," I said. "Do you have another one?"

Mom shook her head. "Abuelita would never throw that away. She'll tell you every crack has a story behind it."

Abuelita smiled. "Your cousin Elena dropped it when she was playing waitress a few years ago," she said. "Now I will always remember that day." She held the cracked dish to her chest and then handed it to me.

I took it carefully and turned toward the kitchen. After some searching, I finally found the box of sugar on top of the refrigerator. As I was pouring the sugar cubes into the bowl, my tablet dinged. *A message!* I reached for my tablet, excited to find out which cousin had written to me.

'Are you in Chile right now?' the message read, followed by about a hundred question marks.

But it wasn't from Julieta, Elena, Bastian, or Hugo. It was from Claire Jacobs, a girl I knew from the youth astronaut training program I did over the summer. I had told her I'd be in Chile for winter break.

'Yep. I'm here!' I typed back, a little disappointed to be chatting with Claire instead of my cousins. After all, being so friendly with Claire was something still new to me. We hadn't been exactly the best of friends at the training program.

In fact, I had thought I could *never* be friends with her after the pool incident at camp, when she left me trapped in an underwater closet during a scuba diving mission. I had frantically pounded on the door for help, but Claire had already gone back to the surface and left me behind—alone. We had learned that abandoning your partner during a mission was one of the worst things you could do. Luckily, our scuba instructor rescued me and helped me swim to safety.

At the end of camp, Claire apologized for what she did, and even helped me when I panicked during another dive by teaching me a trick to calm down. But I still didn't consider her my friend. So I was really surprised when she messaged me a few weeks into the school year, acting like nothing had happened. Still, I had messaged her back, because no matter how mixed up I felt about our friendship, I thought I should give Claire a second chance.

DING! DING! Claire sent another message: a bunch of emojis, half of which I'd never seen before, like a smiling heart walking a dog and an animated rocket launching into space and a flapping Chilean flag. And then: 'Guess what?!'

I sent back a zebra-striped question mark.

'We're flying to Chile right this minute!' Claire messaged. 'Me and my dad!'

'What?' I typed back. 'Like, right now?'

'My dad has a meeting in the Atacama Desert and no one is around to watch me since it's winter break. So I have to come with him,' she replied.

Claire's dad was famous space entrepreneur Lance Jacobs, whose company built their own rockets.

'My dad said you could come with us,' Claire messaged. 'Want to come? Please? Please? Please?'

"Luci?" Mom called from the patio. "*Necesitamos el azúcar.*" The sugar! I had almost forgotten.

"Okay!" I called, closing up the box of sugar cubes and stashing it back on top of the refrigerator. A loose cube rolled off the counter and crunched under my shoe.

Go to the Atacama Desert? With Claire? To be honest, I just wanted to hang out with my cousins. How would they feel if I took off with a girl who wasn't really my friend before I even got to catch them all up on my adventures?

My tablet dinged again. 'We'll stay a couple of nights in the Mars habitat!'

That got my attention.

'Are you serious?' I wrote back.

"Luci!" Mom called again.

I grabbed the sugar bowl. "Coming!" I said, and hustled outside.

As soon as I put the bowl in the middle of the table, Abuelita motioned for me to take a seat next to her. But I was desperate to return to my tablet in the kitchen. "I got some sugar on the floor," I said, giving an excuse to go back inside. "I'll be right back. *¡Un momento!*" I spun toward the kitchen.

Claire had already responded. 'There are NASA scientists living in the habitat now but they're almost finished with their research mission, so Dad said it's okay if we go.'

'No way!' I wrote back, feeling a rush of excitement zing down my spine. Hanging out with real NASA scientists in a Mars habitat in the middle of the desert? How could I pass up that kind of invitation?

"Luciana," I heard Abuelita call. "Come now. We're waiting for you."

'Let me talk to my parents,' I quickly typed back, and then hurried out to the patio.

"Guess who's coming to Chile?" I said, sitting next to Abuelita. "Claire."

Dad frowned and Mom clicked her tongue. "She is the girl that left Luci underwater," she said to Abuelita.

"Oh, yes, I heard about this." Abuelita shook her head. "Terrible. Just terrible."

"She apologized," I explained. "And we've kept in touch."

"Luciana is trying to build a friendship with this girl now," Mom said to Abuelita, sitting back in her chair and sipping her tea. She pressed her lips together, signaling her disapproval.

"Mom," I said. "It's okay to give people second chances. That's what Abuelita always says." Abuelita smiled at me.

"What she did was put your life at risk," Mom said quietly. Dad nodded next to her.

Maybe this wasn't a good time to bring up Claire's

invitation to the Mars habitat. Besides, the truth was I still had nightmares about being trapped in the underwater closet. And sometimes when I was in a small place or in a tight squeeze, I panicked, my brain spinning with the same fear I felt in that pool. Maybe I *didn't* want to be in the middle of the desert with Claire.

Abuelita poured me some warm tea, adding two sugar cubes to make it extra sweet, the way I liked it. "It's up to our Luci to decide whether she wants to stay friends with this Claire," she said to my parents, smiling at me. "Don't worry, *mi niña*. You'll figure it out."

"Thank you, Abuelita," I said, slurping my tea.

"What a wonderful week we're going to have," Abuelita said, changing the subject. "I have been waiting for this visit for so long."

"Me too," I said. My parents both agreed. And for a moment, I just took it all in: the sweet smells of the fruit preserves, the summer breeze on the patio, the colorful flowers of Abuelita's garden. I loved this place.

So when I heard my tablet *DING! DING!* from inside the house, I knew what to do.

'Can't go,' I wrote back to Claire. 'Family stuff.'

She sent back more emojis, this time a frog and snail

and a banged-up car. None of them were smiling. Clearly, she was disappointed.

'Sorry,' I wrote back. But if I was being honest, I wasn't that sorry because I was finally in Chile with my entire family, and we were going to have a giant asado. As much as I would have loved to spend time in a Mars habitat with real NASA scientists, and even though such an experience might have brought me one step closer to my dream of being the first girl on Mars, this week my mission was just to be with my family.

CHAPTER 3

LOS CUATRO

We spent the rest of the day getting ready for the asado, letting the meat slow-cook for many hours on the *parrilla*, the delicious smells making my mouth water. We peeled potatoes and sliced hundreds of tomatoes and onions for *ensalada a la chilena*. And I barely even thought about NASA scientists and a Mars habitat in the desert.

Barely.

Izzy toddled around, pulling open cabinets and digging into baskets around the house. She brought me an old metal toy car, with chipped red and blue paint.

"Beep beep," she said.

Abuelita turned away from the stove and wiped her forehead. The kitchen was as steamy hot as the potatoes she was boiling. "Ah, that was your papa's car," she said.

"This was Grandpa's?" I asked, handing the toy

over to her. Something that old and special belonged on a high shelf, not in the hands of my little sister, who was now ripping up an empty paper towel roll and throwing bits of cardboard across the floor.

Abuelita picked up Izzy's mess. "Do you remember?" she asked me.

Remember what? I wondered. I didn't remember much about Papa, who died when I was six. Then something sparked in my memory: playing with my grandfather on the living room floor during our last visit to Chile. Papa had constructed a racetrack out of old hardcover books, and I spent hours zooming cars around the track with my cousins. It had been the last time I saw Papa before he died.

"I remember playing with that car. On Papa's racetrack," I said.

Abuelita nodded. She kissed the car and handed it back to me.

I held it close to my heart, trying to remember more about that day, and about Papa. I remembered his rough mustache and his clothes that smelled like coffee and cigars. I lifted the car to my nose, hoping it would still carry Papa's scent, but it only smelled like rusty metal.

I put the car down on the coffee table and lingered over the trinkets lining Abuelita's shelves, wondering about the stories each one told.

Just then, the front door of the house opened and in walked my aunt and uncle with their little Ana, who was Izzy's age. And then a second later, Tía Fanny arrived in her wheelchair, followed by a steady stream of more aunts and uncles and little cousins who filled Abuelita's small cottage and eventually spilled onto the patio. The asado had begun!

Dad piled some food on a tray and handed it to me. I breathed in the smell of Abuelita's *choripanes,* my favorite sandwiches with chorizo sausage on crispy marraqueta bread. Smiling, I headed into the crowd, greeting my family with hugs and kisses and choripanes with a side of Abuelita's homemade spicy *pebre* sauce. My relatives marveled over how much I'd grown and asked me about my astronaut training. As I answered their questions, I scanned the room and the patio for my four cousins. Finally, I asked my uncle Javier where they were.

"*¿Los Cuatro?*" he said. "They are looking for you too."

"*¿Los Cuatro?*" I repeated.

"We call them 'The Four' because they are always together," Uncle Javier explained.

Well, maybe I can make it The Five now, I thought.

Uncle Javier took the tray so that I could go find my cousins. I squeezed through the crowd and finally saw four heads huddled together on the couch.

My cousin Julieta popped up. "Astro-Luci!"

Was that what they called me? It was the perfect nickname for a future astronaut, like me. Julieta and Elena scrambled over to hug me. After we let go, I went to hug the boys, Bastian and Hugo. But it was obvious that hugging my boy cousins wasn't cool, so I gave them a weird fist bump/handshake thing and then sat down next to Julieta.

"We have missed you!" Julieta said, hooking her elbow to mine. Her Spanish was faster than Abuelita's. "We have lots of stories to tell you!"

"Me too," I said. "So much has happened!" And then, it was like I couldn't wait a second longer and I filled them in on everything: how I had been the captain of the robotics team at Space Camp and how there was a counselor there with a robotic unicycle and a giant talking dinosaur in his office. And I told them that I won a spot on the scuba team to conduct a mission on the ocean floor.

"*Wait*," Elena stopped me. "You scuba dived to the bottom of the ocean?"

I nodded. "And I slept down there in an underwater habitat called Cetus! It was so cool. You would have loved it there!"

Julieta shook her head. "No. No, thank you. That sounds terrifying!"

"It was a little scary," I agreed with her. But my cousins all seemed so impressed and proud of me, that I kept the detail about my panic attack to myself. Instead I went on, telling them more about all I had been doing to reach my dream of someday becoming the first kid to go to Mars.

I was in the middle of telling them about the underwater trainer when Hugo yawned, big and loud. Bastian burst out laughing. Elena flapped a hand to shush them, but before long, all four cousins were giggling rather than listening to my stories.

"I almost forgot," I interrupted, trying to ignore the feeling of annoyance that burned in my belly. "I brought you gifts."

"You did?" Bastian asked, perking up.

I reached into my pocket and pulled out the NASA pins that I had individually wrapped for each cousin.

"Open them up," I said.

Bastian ripped off the wrapping paper and stared at the pin. "Oh." His smile looked pasted on. "Thanks." He shot a puzzled look to the rest of the cousins. Hugo whispered something to him that I couldn't hear.

"N-A-S-A," Elena said, leaning over Bastian's shoulder. "The American space agency, right?"

"Yes!" I said, maybe a little too enthusiastically.

The rest of the cousins opened their pin packages, saying thank you and being very polite. Almost *too* polite.

"I got them at Space Camp," I explained, suddenly feeling very self-conscious. "Something to remind you of me when I'm not here, I guess."

"Thank you, Astro-Luci," Elena said. "We love them." Except their faces told me that they thought the pins were boring and weird, which was the opposite of loving it. In fact, they seemed to think my stories were boring too. I had hoped they'd be proud of me, but instead, it was like they were barely even interested. I didn't understand why.

"Want to go to the park?" Julieta announced, breaking the awkward silence.

"Um, you guys go ahead," I said. "I'll meet you there."

Los Cuatro sprung off the couch and headed for the patio, leaving their pins behind on the table. Against my permission, my eyes had filled with tears and I blinked them away furiously.

I tiptoed up to the loft, knowing that if my parents saw me they would tell me I had to come back downstairs and be social. I heard Izzy call, "Lulu!" but I pretended I didn't hear her and continued up the stairs. I flopped on my bed, listening to the asado going on without me and staring at the wall of family photos that didn't include me.

My first encounter with my cousins was a failure. At this point, they were definitely not interested in making me part of their little group. And between the giggling faces and their disappointed reaction to my gift, I was beginning to wonder whether they even liked me. But we were all part of the same family. And family sticks together, right? So why did it feel like I didn't even know them anymore?

Suddenly, I felt a rumbling from underneath me, as if someone was pounding up the loft stairs, urgently and angrily. Was someone coming to bring me back to the party? But when I leapt out of bed and looked through the railing, nobody was there. And the rumbling had turned into a tremble I could feel through my entire body.

CHAPTER 4

TEMBLOR

Mom!" I yelled. The shaking threw me off-balance, and I grabbed the railing. "Mom! Dad!"

The frames on the wall swung on their nails, crashing into each other, some falling to the floor and shattering. And through the grinding noises and thunderous shaking, I could hear Dad call back, "We are coming, Luci!" I clung to the loft railing, hoping he would come quick.

And just as I saw him appear in the family room, the shaking stopped. It hadn't lasted for more than half a minute, but I ran down the stairs and into my dad's arms, grateful it was over.

"*Temblor*," he said.

Earthquake.

Dad led me out into the front yard. The street was already full of people, car alarms blaring.

"*¿Están heridos?*" my aunt called out, asking if anyone was hurt.

Frantically, I looked around for Izzy, relieved to see her safe in Mom's arms.

"Luci, I'm so glad you're okay," Mom said, pulling me in for a hug.

"What do we do now?" I asked. I had never experienced an earthquake before. Would there be another one? Was it safe to go inside?

"Let's get cleaned up," Aunt Lorena said, holding open the front door.

Los Cuatro were rounding up their little brothers and sisters in the yard. I started toward them, but Mom stopped me.

"You can socialize with your cousins later, mi niña. Go help Abuelita in the house."

I found Abuelita in the kitchen, standing over a cake with pink frosting and candy flowers that had fallen to the floor, upside down and cracked in half.

"Oh no!" I said.

Abuelita gave me a gentle smile. "Ah, Lucita, it is terrible to lose a perfectly good cake," she said, "but the important thing is that we're safe. That earthquake could have been so much worse."

"Really?" I asked. Because if you asked me, it had been pretty awful.

She dragged the trash can next to the cake and grabbed a serving spoon and a spatula out of the drawer. Together we scooped the cake into the trash.

"That was only a tremor," she explained, wiping up a streak of icing on the floor. "There have been a lot of those lately. I worry it means the big one—*el terremoto*—is coming."

I had heard that before, that a bunch of tremors could be warnings for a big earthquake. If that had been just a little tremor, I didn't even want to think about what a *terremoto* would feel like. The breeze coming in off the patio gave me goose bumps, even though it was ninety degrees outside.

"When do you think the big one will come?" I asked, rubbing my arms.

Abuelita shrugged. "Maybe never," she said, pulling the bag out of the trash can and tying it closed. "Or maybe tomorrow. We do not know."

When she saw the terrified look on my face, she pulled me close. "There's nothing we can do by worrying, Luci. Earthquakes are part of living in Chile. We can't stop our lives out of fear of the unknown," she said as she kissed my forehead. "Besides, our houses are *muy fuertes*." Very strong.

That made me feel a little better.

Through the open kitchen window I could see Izzy playing with her ball. She tossed it in the air and watched it roll under a rosebush that was bursting with pink flowers—and giant thorns.

"No, Izzy!" I called as she toddled toward the bush. I rushed outside and caught her just before she reached for her ball.

She wailed and I tried to calm her down. "Let me get it, Izzy. Look. Thorns." I carefully pulled the bush back and showed her. But as I did, I saw something that made me snap back: an ugly crack in the foundation of Abuelita's house. Chunks of concrete were sprinkled among the mulch and rose petals.

"Mama! Abuelita!" I called. "Look at this!"

Everyone came running, not just Mom and Abuelita, but the aunts and uncles and even the cousins.

Abuelita covered her mouth in shock when she saw the damage. "Ay, no!" she cried. "How will I fix this?"

As we all stared at the crack, one of my uncles leaned down to touch its rough edges. "Let's get a professional to look at this tomorrow," he said.

Abuelita nodded, but remained silent. There was a flurry of discussion around her from the rest of the family about how deep the crack went and how much it would cost to fix and whether it was even safe for us to stay in the house overnight.

Mom put her arm around Abuelita. "Let's not panic yet. Maybe it's an easy repair."

"And now that we know there's a problem," Dad said, "we can fix it before it grows bigger."

Abuelita wiped a tear from her cheek. Mom and Aunt Lorena put their arms around Abuelita's shoulders, and then Izzy and I hugged Mom, and soon almost everyone was linked together in one big hug in front of the rosebush.

And even though Los Cuatro had joined in the group hug just a few feet away from me, it felt like they were a world away.

It seemed it wasn't only Abuelita's cottage that was damaged. And what if the damage was so great, it was already beyond repair?

Then what? What would become of my mission to get to know my family? And just as important, what would become of our family home?

Chapter 5

MISSION FAILURE

The next day, the inspector arrived just as we finished eating lunch. Julieta's parents, Aunt Lorena and Uncle Panchito, had come over to Abuelita's with little Mica, who was playing with Izzy. Bastian's parents were there too, but Los Cuatro were nowhere to be seen—more proof that my mission to catch up with my cousins wasn't going so well.

We followed the inspector outside. Dad carefully pulled the rosebush aside and the inspector knelt down to take a closer look at the foundation. He had some kind of measuring tool and he wrote down a lot of numbers. Mom rolled the ball back and forth with Izzy and Mica, watching the inspector over her shoulder. Abuelita paced around the yard.

Next, Abuelita escorted him down to the basement. I waited outside with everybody else, hoping that there would be an easy fix.

Soon the inspector reappeared on the patio. Abuelita stood behind him, looking glum. The inspector stared at his clipboard and spoke quietly in Spanish. He used a lot of big technical words that I didn't understand, but I could tell right away from his soft and careful voice that the news was not great. I caught a few phrases that I understood: "quite a serious crack" and "house is not stable" and "very expensive." And then he said, "If there is a *terremoto*, you will not be safe here. I recommend that you find another place to stay."

I could barely look at Abuelita, who was now hugging my mom and the rest of the aunts, her hand to her heart.

"I wish I had better news," the inspector said, ripping off a sheet of paper from his book and handing it to Abuelita.

When the inspector left, we lingered in the living room, the aunts sitting on the couch with Abuelita while Dad and the uncles went back into the basement to check out what the inspector saw.

"This house," Abuelita said, wiping her eyes, speaking low. "It has been in our family for so long. This is where I raised my babies." She squeezed Mom's hand. "And where my mama raised *her* babies."

"I know, Mamita," Mom said. She cleared her throat like she was trying not to cry.

I thought of all of the pictures I had seen in the loft. Most of the photos had been taken in this house. I'd seen photos of at least three weddings that had taken place on this very patio. A photo of my own mom doing her homework at the kitchen table when she was my age.

Abuelita reached out and touched the walls of the cottage. "This house is more than just a home. It's our oldest living family member." She took a shaky breath. "How can I leave this place? This house is the heart of our family." And for a second I couldn't breathe because Abuelita—who never cried, not even when she broke her pinky toe on our coffee table during her last visit to Virginia—had tears welling in her eyes.

I sat in one of the armchairs, the upholstery worn thin on the arms from years of other relatives sitting here. Papa. My great-grandma. Maybe even my great-great-grandma. I looked up at Abuelita. I couldn't find the words to make her feel better, and I certainly couldn't save her house myself. I wished there was something—anything—I could do.

"Luci," Mom called, as if she were reading my thoughts. "Can you run over to Aunt Lorena's house and grab some of the empty boxes in her garage?" That was Julieta's house, on the other side of the park. "We're going to start packing Abuelita's things."

I stood up, grateful to be helpful in some way. "Okay, I'll go." And then I raced out the door and across the park to Aunt Lorena's house. When I got there, I was surprised to find Los Cuatro standing in the driveway.

"Hey," I said, trying to forget the awkward reunion we'd had the night before. Today was a new day. A new chance at my mission.

My cousins looked up. "Astro-Luci!" Julieta said. "What's the news on Abuelita's house?"

"Not good." As I explained what the inspector had told us, my cousins' smiles faded.

"That's terrible," Elena said. The others nodded.

"I'm just here for some boxes so we can pack up a few things for Abuelita. Do you know where your mom keeps her empty boxes?"

She pointed to the garage, where I saw a pile of cardboard boxes stacked up in the corner.

"Oh, and my family and I might be staying here with you tonight," I added because we couldn't sleep at Abuelita's anymore and I knew Julieta's house had a guest room. Suddenly, I felt a little hopeful. Maybe this would be my chance to connect with my cousins at last.

Julieta looked up. "Oh, that would be fun. The thing is . . ." she trailed off.

The look on her face made my heart sink. Was she going to disinvite me from staying at her house now?

"We have plans," Bastian blurted.

I stood upright. "Are you going somewhere?"

Elena pulled a duffel bag out of the garage. "One of our friends is having a campout."

"And all of you are going?" I asked. As in, they were all leaving me?

They nodded, and I just stood there awkwardly, not sure what else to say. "Oh," I finally said, forcing a smile. Why did I give up my plans—the kind of plans that involved real-life NASA scientists doing real-life Mars experiments—to spend time with my cousins when they clearly didn't care to do the same?

"I'm sorry, Luci," Julieta said, giving me a stiff pat on the shoulder. "It's just that we've been planning this for a while."

"We're going to celebrate Julieta's big award," Elena said, knocking her hip into Julieta, who was blushing.

"Award?" I said.

What kind of award? When did that happen? Why did it feel like nobody told me about stuff anymore?

I was failing at my mission, which was not my usual style. If I was on a mission to dock a capsule to the Space Station like I did at Space Camp, or to take sand samples from the bottom of the ocean like I did at youth astronaut training camp, I would have done everything to complete the task. To make things work. Why was this so much harder?

"What about tomorrow?" I blurted out. "Want to go to a water park or something?" It was a desperate attempt to save my mission. To be a part of my own family.

My cousins looked at one another.

"Okay. Maybe," Elena said.

"It's just, we're not sure when we'll be back," Julieta added, playing with her necklace. Then she perked up and looked to the other cousins. "Maybe Luci could come with us to the sleepover?"

Out of the corner of my eye, I caught Hugo wince. Elena nudged him.

"She won't know anyone," Bastian said quickly to Julieta.

He was right. But the way he said it—like bringing

me along for the campout was a ridiculous suggestion—made me feel even worse. And what was with Hugo and Elena? Was I embarrassing to them?

Elena put a hand on my arm. "Don't listen to Bastian. If you want to come, then you should come." But it was not like she was begging me.

My skin prickled with awkwardness. Just a few days ago, I would have jumped at the chance to go to a campout with my cousins. But now? No, *gracias*.

"Nah," I said, trying to look like it was no big deal. "Actually, I already have plans. Kind of secret stuff. There might even be some real astronaut scientists involved." I felt my cheeks turn hot. What was I even talking about?

And then I grabbed the pile of boxes and marched back across the park to Abuelita's cottage. My cousins didn't even try to stop me.

Mission failure.

When I got back to the house, Abuelita and my parents were in the loft, wrapping up the unbroken pictures from the wall to pack them away. I climbed upstairs and slumped onto the air mattress.

"Luci, what happened?" Mom asked.

I crossed my arms. "Los Cuatro are leaving to go to a campout tonight."

Abuelita turned from the bookshelf. "Oh, niña, *lo siento.*"

"Don't be sorry, Abuelita," I said. "They said I could go with them, but I thought it would be weird since I don't know any of their friends." I blew a strand of hair out of my face. "They said they're celebrating Julieta and some kind of award. Why am I so out of the loop?" I flopped back on my bed.

"I told you about that," Mom said. "Julieta won an award for her photography."

"You did?" I said, sitting back up.

"Last week at breakfast," Dad insisted. "Maybe you weren't listening."

I crossed my arms again, ignoring that last comment. "It's just I turned down going to the Atacama Desert with Claire because I wanted to spend time with my cousins and now—"

"Wait, what?" Mom said.

"Remember I told you that Claire's in Chile?" I asked. "She and her dad invited me to stay with them in the Mars habitat, where real NASA scientists are actually working."

"They let kids hang out around NASA scientists while they work?" Dad asked.

I shrugged. "Claire's dad said it was okay."

"Well, it's probably for the best that you turned her down," Mom said. She put down a stack of picture frames and faced me. "Sweetheart, we just had an earthquake. We don't know if another one will come, and I don't want you so far away from us if it does."

I sighed. "But Abuelita says we will never know if or when another earthquake is coming. She told me that we can't stop our lives out of fear of the unknown."

Mom and Dad shared a look before glancing at Abuelita. She shrugged innocently and gave me a wink.

Mom turned back to me. "Actually, I'm also concerned about you going anywhere with Claire Jacobs." Dad nodded.

"She's changed a lot since camp," I told them, although I wasn't one hundred percent sure. "We've been messaging for a while and it seems like she's trying really hard to be my friend. I think I can trust her."

"And you would trust this girl enough to follow her into the desert?" Dad asked.

"Dad," I said. "I'd get to sleep in a Mars habitat."

He seemed unconvinced.

"And hang out with NASA scientists," I added. "This is a great opportunity."

Mom and Dad both loved "opportunities."

"Like, a really *rare* opportunity," I added because if my parents loved "opportunities," they especially loved "rare opportunities."

Mom sat down next to me on the bed. "Oh, Luci. I don't know."

"It's just for two nights," I said, pleading my case. "Barely even two full days. I don't want to pass this up."

Mom sighed. "You know that we'd do anything to support your dream to become an astronaut." I held my breath. Was she breaking down? "We just want you to really think about this."

"I have thought about it, Mom," I said. "I want to do this."

Mom and Dad looked at each other, but didn't say a word. Mom smiled at me.

I leapt off the bed, because that was as close to a "yes" as I was going to get. I was going to the Mars habitat! I did a twirly dance, careful not to spin into the picture frames that were left hanging on the wall.

I stopped spinning and looked up at Abuelita. She was smiling, but it was the kind of smile that didn't make it all the way to her eyes.

"Wait," I said. "I can't leave the family right now. Abuelita's house—"

"Isn't going anywhere," Abuelita interrupted. "We are your family," she said. "You can go and come back. We'll still be here with all of the problems." She patted my shoulder and headed for the loft stairs. "In fact, I have something for you."

She disappeared downstairs, and when she returned a second later, she was carrying something small in her hand.

"See? You can take a piece of the family with you."

I kissed her cheek.

It was Papa's little toy car.

CHAPTER 6

A NEW MISSION

I messaged Claire and told her I had changed my mind, crossing my fingers that she and her dad hadn't already left for the desert. Luckily, Mr. Jacobs had a meeting in Santiago and they weren't leaving for the Atacama until that afternoon. So, just a few hours after I got Claire's message, Mom, Dad, Abuelita, Izzy, and I piled into the car, and drove to the airport to meet Mr. Jacobs's helicopter. Wedged in the back seat between me and Izzy's car seat was a small duffel bag stuffed full with clothes, a few books, a tin of Abuelita's *pan de Pascua*—my favorite Chilean cake—and my grandpa's toy car.

Abuelita drove the car to the back corner of the airport and parked next to the helipad. And as soon as I cracked open my door, Claire ran up to give me a hug as if we were best-best friends. I was surprised at first, but then I hugged her back extra enthusiastically because I knew my parents were watching.

"This is so cool!" she shouted. "I can't believe you can come! My dad even said he'll take us to see the geysers tomorrow morning!" And then she hugged me again, and for a second, I couldn't believe I was standing on a helipad hugging Claire Jacobs, and getting ready to fly to the Atacama Desert. It wasn't exactly what I had expected to be doing during my winter break. But I had a feeling it was going to be an adventure of a lifetime.

A second later, Mr. Jacobs strode over to us, pulling out his earpiece and tucking his phone into the breast pocket of his jacket.

Mr. Jacobs shook my parents' hands. "So good to meet you, Mr. and Mrs. Vega. I will take great care of your daughter during our visit to the habitat. My Claire is so excited to have her with us."

"Thank you, Mr. Jacobs, for inviting her," my mom said.

"Luci is thrilled to be going," Dad added. "Thank you for this rare opportunity."

I stifled a giggle. I knew my parents so well; they really did love rare opportunities.

I was anxious to get moving, so I quickly kissed my parents on their cheeks and then pulled Izzy and Abuelita in for a hug. "I will see you in two days! I love you!" As I walked backward toward the helicopter, Claire linked to my arm, I blew kisses to my little sister. "Mwah! Mwah!" Izzy pretended to catch each one.

For a moment, I felt a wave of regret as I walked away from my family. I knew Los Cuatro were going on a campout, but maybe I had aborted my mission to get to know them too soon. Maybe I should have gone along with my cousins, even if I thought I'd feel left out. But no, I knew I was doing the right thing for me by going along with Claire. This was really a once-in-a-lifetime experience. I patted the outside of my bag to make sure Papa's toy car was there, and then turned to wave goodbye to my family one more time.

The wind from the spinning rotors was strong, and I had to duck as I followed Claire and her dad to the helicopter. As I hopped inside, I hung on to the door, which, by the way, felt pretty flimsy for a door that was the only thing keeping me from falling thousands of feet out of the sky. Claire motioned that I should take the seat next to the window.

"Are you sure you don't want the window?" I asked.

She shook her head vigorously, and I remembered that she had told me at training camp that she was afraid of flying, especially in helicopters.

"Are you going to be okay?" I asked her. It was an unfortunate fear for her to have since her dad mostly traveled by helicopter. But I could kind of understand why she was so afraid when I saw how tight the space was inside the helicopter. There wasn't any room to walk around, not like on the airplane we had taken to Chile. It was hard to believe this tiny pod would be taking us up thousands of feet in the air.

"I'll be okay," Claire said. "Thanks, Luci."

I smiled at her, happy that I decided to come. Happy that I was giving her a second chance. This wasn't the same Claire that left me behind in the pool last summer. I could tell from all our messages back and forth, and now from seeing her in person, that she was a different girl outside of the training program. It was like the pressure of making the dive team had been too much for her, and caused her to act all mean and irresponsible.

Mr. Jacobs was the last one in the helicopter, hoisting my duffel onto the front seat next to the pilot, along with the rest of the bags and then hurling himself into the seat next to Claire. The pilot handed us giant headphones with attached microphones, and we each placed them on our heads. And for a minute, it felt like I was back in Space Camp in one of the simulators, communicating to Mission Control through my mouthpiece.

Except this wasn't a simulation. This was a real trip to see real NASA scientists. If I hadn't already been securely buckled in, I might have busted out into a happy dance.

As we took off, I leaned toward the window and waved for as long as I could see my family, accidentally elbowing Claire in the ribs a few times.

"Will you please?" Claire finally said, joking.

I sat back. "Sorry!" I said into my headpiece. I stared out the window until the airport disappeared and the cityscape of Santiago came into view, glowing gold from the setting sun. "How much farther until we get there?"

"Just another 5.9 trillion miles." Mr. Jacobs's voice crackled through my headphones.

Claire rolled her eyes. "Dad, be serious. The Atacama isn't a light-year away."

I felt my face turn hot, not realizing Mr. Jacobs could hear what I said through my microphone.

"Ignore him," Claire said. "He's always saying weird stuff like that."

Mr. Jacobs snorted. "It'll be a while, Luci. Might as well get comfortable."

"Wait until you see this place," Claire said, grinning. "I've been there once and the desert is like nothing else you've ever seen. Although if you're stuck in the Mars habitat while your dad has a meeting it can be boring. But tomorrow we're going to see the geysers. There's a whole field of them, and—"

"Whoa," Mr. Jacobs interrupted, holding up a hand. "Did you just say the Atacama Desert can be boring?"

Claire shook her head. "No, I said, when *you're* not there, the Mars habitat can be—"

"Do you know the kind of work we're doing there?" Mr. Jacobs interrupted again.

Claire smacked her forehead. "Here we go," she said to me, but she was smiling.

"The Atacama Desert is the closest we can get to a real Mars environment here on Earth," Mr. Jacobs began. "It's barren of animals and plants."

"Even snakes?" I asked. I had a mostly-hate relationship with snakes so anyplace without reptiles was my kind of place.

Mr. Jacobs nodded and continued. "The Atacama is

the driest place on Earth. And when scientists compared soil from the Atacama Desert to soil from Mars, it was nearly identical." He took a breath. "Do you know what that means?"

"It means it's the perfect place for astronauts to test their signs of life equipment they'll use on Mars," Claire answered.

"Signs of life?" I said, looking at Claire. "Like . . ."

"Not aliens and stuff," she said. "Microorganisms. Science. Blah-blah-blah."

"We've talked about this, Claire," Mr. Jacobs cautioned. "Microorganisms are not blah-blah-blah. If bacteria and other microorganisms can live in someplace like Mars, then maybe humans can too."

"Cool," I said, feeling goose bumps.

It was like I was embarking on an entirely new mission. An Astro-Luci kind of mission: to live on a Mars habitat in the middle of the Atacama Desert with real NASA scientists. Maybe I'd even get to do something spectacular while I was there, which would definitely make my family proud. And maybe when my cousins heard about what I had done, they'd be so impressed they'd let me into their little circle. Maybe then we could be The Five.

After a couple of hours, I noticed we were leaving behind the sprinkling of lights from the Chilean towns below us, and disappearing into a void of blackness.

"Is that the desert? Are we here?" I asked, my head pressed against the window.

It looked like we were flying over an ocean. No lights below. No landmarks. We could have been flying over a giant ravine, or a canyon that was created by an asteroid hit. There was nothing below—just blackness.

Mr. Jacobs peered out the window. "We're not at the habitat yet, but yes, that is the Atacama."

I looked over at Claire. She had started taking long, deep breaths and I wondered if she was feeling scared. If it was Raelyn, my best friend from home, sitting next to me, I would have grabbed her hand or given her a hug and Rae would have done the same for me. But it was Claire, and despite her hugs from before, Claire and I weren't exactly in a best-friend situation. Yet.

"Hey," I said, nudging Claire.

Her eyes were shut tight.

Mr. Jacobs patted Claire on the knee. "Just a little

while longer," he said, sitting back in his seat and closing his eyes.

I whispered, "Are you okay?" through the headset.

Claire gave me a thumbs-up, but her clenched jaw told me that she was still afraid.

"Are you doing your trick?" I asked. When I panicked in the underwater habitat at the training program, Claire had tried to calm me down by asking me to tell her three things that I saw, three things I could feel, and three things I could smell. And the trick actually worked.

She nodded, her eyes closed in concentration.

Soon a spotlight flicked on from underneath the helicopter, illuminating the ground below. All I could see was reddish dirt, and then a white pod came into view. Mr. Jacobs sat up, rubbed his eyes, and stared out the window. "There's the habitat."

My heart beat faster, and I got goose bumps again.

I shook Claire, barely able to contain myself. We were here.

CHAPTER 7

ATACAMA DESERT

The helicopter hovered a few feet above a clear spot on the sand, and slowly lowered. We landed with a bump, and once the captain gave us the okay, we tore off our headsets and dropped out the side door. I ducked under the rotors and pulled my shirt over my mouth and nose like Mr. Jacobs and Claire did to avoid the swirling desert dust, which had been kicked up by the helicopter.

Mr. Jacobs turned on a flashlight so we could see our way to the habitat, but the moon and stars above were so bright that we almost didn't need his light to navigate over the rocky terrain. I stopped for a moment to gaze at the sky, and Claire crashed into me.

"Oh, sorry," I said. "But look up."

Claire craned her neck, and we both took in the biggest and brightest night sky I had ever seen in my life.

"Wow," I whispered. "Just wow."

"Let's go, girls," Mr. Jacobs called.

Claire pulled me toward the habitat, where the glow of the soft lights from inside poured out the windows and onto the dark desert ground. No signs of life. Except for us.

The Mars habitat was a white cylinder on legs, with modules sticking out on all sides. We walked past a tented area set up like a laboratory, and I slowed down so I could take a better look inside, but Claire grabbed my hand, urging me to move ahead. We walked up a wide ramp to the first module, where Mr. Jacobs held the door for us, our bags slung over his arm. As I looked back over my shoulder at the desert, I could actually imagine being on Mars.

We stepped inside and Mr. Jacobs pushed the door closed against the gusty wind. "Welcome to the airlock," he said. "If we were in space this is where the astronauts would come and go for their EVAs, or space walks. Both doors are sealed so when this one is open to space"—he pointed to the door we just came from—"it doesn't contaminate the entire habitat."

Claire waited impatiently by the other door.

"We really only have to worry about dust here, though," he said, motioning Claire forward. We each grabbed our bags, stomping our feet on a mat, and stepped through the door that led to the main module of the habitat.

Two women and a man were sitting at a table and they looked up and smiled as we entered. "Lance!" the man said. And then they were all shaking hands and hugging Mr. Jacobs like they were long-lost buddies.

Claire and I stood next to Mr. Jacobs and I thought, *How cool would it be to have a dad that was friends with a bunch of NASA scientists?*

"I was hoping you'd come!" one of the women said, hugging Claire. "Did you have a nice Christmas?" She nudged Mr. Jacobs. "Did you get her that telescope I was telling you about?"

"I got a new computer instead," Claire said, the lady giving Mr. Jacobs a disapproving look. "But I downloaded the app to track Curiosity."

I knew about that app. You could actually see where the Mars rover, Curiosity, was at any moment. The lady smirked at Claire. "Well, okay. I guess that's better than nothing." And then she turned to me. "And who is this?"

"This is my friend Luciana Vega," Claire said.

"It's so nice to meet you, Luciana," the scientist replied. "My name is Vanessa Rife."

She was wearing a blue shirt that said CETUS PROGRAM on it and I caught my breath. "Have you been to Cetus?" I asked her.

She looked down at her shirt. "Oh! Do you know Cetus? Wait, did you go to the training camp with Claire?"

I nodded.

"She was on the dive team," Claire said, smiling at me. "She was awesome."

I looked at Claire with surprise, knowing how much she had wanted a spot on that team herself. "Thanks, Claire." It really meant a lot coming from her, considering everything that happened at camp. See? I was right. Claire was so different than the girl I knew at camp, and that was why I believed in giving people second chances.

Vanessa clapped her hands together. "Yes! I know exactly who you are! I saw your name in the log book. *Luciana, future first girl to Mars.*"

I blushed and stuffed my hands in my pockets. There was a log book on the underwater habitat, and if you made the dive team and visited Cetus, you got to sign the book. That's what I had written next to my name: *future first girl to Mars.*

"I had a dream when I was your age too," Vanessa said, and then she opened up her arms and motioned around the habitat. "It took some work, but here I am." She came in closer. "Don't ever let anyone tell you that you can't make it happen."

The guy next to her snorted. "Your dream was to live in a tin can in the middle of the desert for ten days?"

Vanessa smacked him on the shoulder, and then he extended his hand to me. "Rick Paige. And it's very nice to meet you." And then he whispered, "I was just kidding. This place is awesome."

"My name is Pia," the third scientist said. "I am a geologist from a nearby university, Universidad de Antofagasta." She smiled at me. "*¿Chilena?*" She pointed from me to her. She was Chilean too.

"Sí," I said.

"*Bienvenidas.* Welcome," she said to me and Claire. "Want a tour of this place?"

"Yes, please!" I said, with a little too much enthusiasm.

The habitat had three modules. We were standing in the main core, where Mr. Jacobs and the other two scientists were now sitting around the table. There was a robotics and science lab module attached at one end and a hygiene module at the other end. The hygiene module is what most people would call a bathroom. But since we were out in the middle of the desert and there was no running water, we had an incinerating toilet and sponge bath station instead. For the first time, I was actually a little relieved that we'd only be here for two nights.

The core module was two stories high. The galley, which is what the kitchen is called, and the communication station were on the first floor.

Pia told us where to find the fire extinguisher, satellite phones, flashlights, and the first aid kit. "In case you find yourselves in trouble," she said.

We're only going to be here for a day and a half, I thought to myself. *How much trouble could we get into?*

Then Pia pointed to a ladder that would bring us up to the crew quarters at the top of the cupola, the tall domed structure. Claire and I would share a sleeping pod, which was big enough for a narrow bunk bed, squeezed against the cushioned walls.

"Cozy," Claire said, and I felt my stomach flip. Tight spaces made me nervous.

"How about you take the bottom bunk?" Claire suggested. "We'll keep the curtain to our pod open, okay?" She helped me wedge my duffel at the foot of my bed. "And look, there's a window." She pointed to the ceiling outside our sleep quarters and I noticed the cupola, a dome of windows at the top of the habitat.

We said good night to the scientists and put on our pajamas. Claire climbed up to her bed, and before long, I heard her soft snoring. For the first time all day, I felt a flicker of homesickness. I pulled out my grandpa's toy car, and thought about Abuelita sleeping in one of my aunts' guest rooms rather than in her own bed. I cradled the car against my chest and settled in, digging myself under my blankets.

From my bed, I could see trillions of stars in the sky twinkling through the windows of the cupola.

And even though I was really in a tin can in the middle of the Atacama Desert, I had never in my entire life felt so close to being in space.

CHAPTER 8

IOU

The next morning when we got up, we climbed down the ladder to the first floor. Claire headed straight over to the table in the core module, where her dad was sitting, and gave him a big kiss on the cheek.

Mr. Jacobs barely looked up, absorbed in what he was doing.

The scientists looked busy too, all hunched over a map at one of the worktables.

"Good morning, sleepyheads," Rick said, finally noticing that we were there.

"Buenos días," Pia said, her mouth full of the banana she was eating.

Claire and I waved and then shuffled over to the galley area for some breakfast.

"We should eat fast," Claire said to me, "so we don't miss the geysers, right, Dad?" she called across the room. "They're only active in the morning. Hey, do you like Fruit-eee-ohs? It's my favorite cereal to eat when I'm in Chile." She pulled a fluorescent box down from the cabinet with cartoony fruit all over it.

"Sure," I said. I was a little disappointed that we wouldn't be eating space food, like the dehydrated shrimps in little silver packets that we ate on Cetus. But eating cereal while watching the scientists take notes and tap different areas of their map would be pretty cool too. I wondered what they were planning to do today.

"They'll be here when we get back, don't worry," Claire said with a laugh, catching me peering at the scientists. She handed me a bowl of cereal and a spoon and we sat down. "They're probably going on a sampling run. That's what they do here. Sample dirt and stuff."

"Yeah, but they're basically practicing to look for aliens," I said, trying to overhear what the scientists were saying, and accidentally dribbling some milk and a few Fruit-eee-ohs onto my lap.

"Well, if you think that's cool," Claire said, "just wait until you see the geysers."

I took a big spoonful of cereal. "Yep. I can't wait." But I imagined going back to Santiago and telling my cousins all about my trip: "We stayed in a space habitat, and while the scientists looked for mysterious life-forms, we ate cereal and watched water shoot out of the ground instead!"

Not exactly impressive.

I was slurping up the last of my cereal when we heard a helicopter outside.

"Time for geysers!" Claire sang, hopping out of her seat so fast she nearly dumped her cereal bowl on the floor.

Mr. Jacobs stood up, collecting his things, stuffing them into a bag, and staring at his watch. "Anyone need anything in Antofagasta?"

Claire froze. "Dad?"

"I had a meeting pop up, but I shouldn't be long." Mr. Jacobs swung his bag onto his shoulder, and walked across the room to kiss Claire on the forehead.

"But we're supposed to do a geyser tour this morning, right?" Claire said.

Mr. Jacobs stopped and smacked his forehead, rubbing his face with his hand. "I'm sorry, Claire. Can we reschedule? Consider it an official IOU."

Claire's body sunk, and I thought she might burst into tears. But I knew crying was very un-Claire-like.

"Claire," he said before she could really react, or talk back, "you know how I feel."

"Yeah," she said, rolling her eyes. "Work is the most important thing in your life."

I couldn't help glancing at Claire when I heard that biting comment. She sounded like the old Claire, the one who left me trapped in an underwater closet at camp. She even *looked* like the old Claire: hip jutted out, eyes squinted, face scrunched into a scowl.

"That's not true," her dad said, looking between Claire and the door. "You know that you come before everything. You're my daughter, my one and only."

Claire sighed. "I am not a kid anymore, Dad. In fact, you can keep your IOU because I've got enough of those already."

And with that, she stomped up the ladder to the crew quarters.

Mr. Jacob groaned. "Okay, I'll have to deal with this when I get back or else I'll be late to my meeting." He looked at the scientists. "The girls will be fine here, so don't feel like you have to watch over them. I'll be back before nightfall." And then he turned to me. "Please tell Claire I love her." And with a wave, he was gone.

I felt badly for Claire, but a part of me was happy to stay here and spend more time around the scientists. Except, as soon as Mr. Jacobs left, the scientists rolled up their map and started collecting their things.

"Are we ready to go?" Pia asked the crew.

Rick nodded and patted his pocket where his phone stuck out. "We've got our coordinates."

"Great. Let me load up the suits," Vanessa said, and then she ducked into the airlock.

I stood there, not wanting to interrupt, but I really, really wanted to go with them, wherever they were going. And I really, *really* didn't want to be stuck here with Claire, who was clearly in a rotten mood.

"Where are you guys going?" I finally asked.

Pia looked up from the bag she was sorting through. "It's our last day of sampling. We have one more site we want to hit before we leave. We need to collect samples for the university in Antofagasta."

My stomach twisted with nerves. Would they ask me to tag along?

But no one said anything to me; the scientists just picked up their bags and maps and water bottles and hats and walked out of the core module.

I thought about my new mission, and how I was

supposed to be making my family proud out here. How could I go home and tell them that I just sat doing nothing in a Mars habitat in the middle of the desert for a bunch of boring hours?

I decided I wasn't ready to give up on this once-in-a-lifetime trip to the Atacama Desert, so I followed the scientists outside.

They were all bustling around a jeep, stacking things on the roof rack, adding coolers and shovels and sampling supplies to the trunk, attaching a trailer to the jeep's hitch.

"Do you need help?" I asked, loud enough for them to hear me over the wind.

The scientists stopped what they were doing and looked up at me standing there on the ramp.

"Uh, I mean . . ." I started to change my mind. What kind of help could a twelve-year-old kid offer to a team of NASA scientists?

"Can you fill up my water bottle, please?" Vanessa asked as she smiled and tossed me the bottle.

I caught it, and I knew it was a tiny job in the scheme of things, but it was a job nonetheless. I walked back inside and I waited until the water from the spigot came out really cold before I filled the bottle. Maybe Vanessa wouldn't notice the cold, refreshing water, but then again, maybe she would.

When I passed the ladder leading to the second floor of the habitat, I called up to Claire, "I'm helping the scientists get ready for their mission if you want to come down!"

She didn't answer, not that I was surprised.

I brought Vanessa the water, and jumped to attention as the scientists gave me more mini jobs to do. I was helping Pia coil a rope when Claire appeared in the doorway of the airlock, her face still pinched in a grimace. I knew it was no use talking to her since she was clearly still in a bad mood. And now I worried that if the scientists didn't take me along, I'd be stuck here with the same kind of Claire I knew from summer camp. The kind of Claire that abandoned her teammates.

It was now or never.

"Pia?" I started. "Do you think you'll need any help wherever you're going?" I crossed my fingers, hoping that I'd proven myself somewhat helpful.

She picked up the bundle of rope. "You want to come along?"

Claire stomped down the ramp. "We have to stay here, Luci. I want to wait for my dad."

I slumped. "Like, all day? Just stay here?" Instead of going on a mission to find signs of life with a team of really cool scientists? Did that even make sense?

And then from around the habitat came Rick—and a rover the size of a golf cart with off-road tires that were almost up to my waist. I was sure my mouth dropped open because Pia nudged me with a laugh.

"Please—can we go with you because I've never seen a rover that cool in my life?" I blurted.

"Well, what do you guys think?" Pia asked the other two scientists. "Do we have room for two little helpers?"

Rick stood up from where he was chaining the rover to the trailer, and then there was a pause that I pretended not to notice. The scientists exchanged glances.

"I promise Claire and I are really good at helping," I said, ignoring Claire's eye rolling. "And we won't get in the way."

And then Vanessa said, "I'm pretty sure we have room for a helper or two," and my heart swelled to double its size.

Until I saw Claire's face, which had turned bright red.

"No. I'm not going. My dad said I could stay here."

She shot me a look, and I knew this was some kind of test, like a friendship test.

Under normal circumstances, I'd have no choice but to stay back with Claire because friends don't leave friends alone in the middle of the desert. Plus, I was her guest here, and staying back would be the polite thing to do.

Except this was far from a regular situation and if Claire was my true friend, she'd know how I wanted to be the first girl to Mars and she'd say, "Okay, we can play board games later, and I'll go into the desert so you can hang out with real NASA scientists."

But maybe that was the problem. We weren't really friends after all.

"Don't you want to see what it's like out there, Claire?" I asked.

"Sure," she said. "By helicopter. With my dad."

"You don't even like heli—" I started to say but Claire cut me off with an icy glare.

"We can put this back seat up," Rick said, pointing to the jeep. "You two should come. Check it out. See what kind of work we're doing."

"I'll even let you guys take a sample for me," Pia offered.

A sample? I thought. *Please, Claire!*

"We also have new Mars prototype astronaut suits to try out," Vanessa added.

"Please, Claire?" I begged out loud this time, grabbing her arm. "Samples and astronaut suits. Those are practically all of my favorite things!"

She pulled out of my grip and crossed her arms again, and I hoped that she'd give in. And she finally did. "Fine. But for the record, I don't want to go."

"Thank-you-thank-you-thank-you!" I sang, giving her a hug.

And it didn't even bother me that she didn't hug me back, because I was going on a mission with NASA scientists. I couldn't wait to tell my cousins about this when I got home.

CHAPTER 9

DESERT MISSION

Once the rover was safely loaded onto the trailer and all of the equipment properly stowed and tied down, we climbed into the jeep. Vanessa drove and Pia used a laptop that had a fancy spiraled antenna coming out of one of its ports to navigate. Rick shared the back seat with some equipment and Claire and I sat on a little bench jump seat in the far back, just big enough for two kids and a small cooler that would be used to hold the samples.

And then we were off, rock music blaring, across the barren Atacama Desert.

The drive to the sampling site took two hours, and Claire didn't talk to me the entire time. I spent most of the ride thinking about how amazing it would be if we found signs of life in the sample Pia let me take. What if my sample was the most important find of their whole mission or something? I'd be *Luciana Vega, expert alien discoverer.* Then NASA would *have* to put me on the first mission to Mars.

A big bump jolted me out of my daydream, and I made eye contact with Claire, who just scowled. It was like the longer we drove, the more irritated she became. And I realized how little I knew her. Which Claire was the real Claire? The mean and selfish Claire from camp? Or the nice Claire that messaged back and forth with me, and was so excited that I was coming with her to the desert in the first place?

When we finally reached the sampling site, the scientists hopped out, stretching their backs and arms and pulling down the seat so Claire and I could easily climb out. And then they started unloading the equipment.

I tried tugging a folding canopy off the roof, but it wouldn't budge. Claire shook her head and walked away, but Pia and Vanessa helped me yank the canopy bag down and we decided to set up the tent right next to the jeep. I helped as much as I could, pulling the legs one way while they pulled another, and a few minutes later, we had a fully functioning sun shelter. While they staked the tent down so it wouldn't get blown away, I dumped all the camping chairs from their carry bags and unfolded them. One knocked over right at Claire's feet, and she looked in the other direction, clearly unwilling to help pick it up.

Vanessa appeared under the canopy, her white shirt already turned a rust color from the blowing desert dust. She pushed her hair out of her face, which was sweaty and streaked with the same red dirt. "I need you two to stay here, all right?" she said. "We're unloading the rover, and then we'll get set up for sampling. These samples are going to the university for more testing, and we need to be very careful to protect them from contamination. If we find a biomarker, or a sign of life, in any of the samples, we want to make sure it came from the soil—and not from one of us."

Claire's face looked like blah-blah-blah, but for real this time. She wasn't messing around.

"Yep. Sure," I said, trying to be extra cheerful to counteract the cloud of grumpiness coming from the chair next to me. "Can I still take a sample, though?"

"Yes," Vanessa said, giving me a thumbs-up. "I will call you over when it's your turn."

"And how will I know if there's a biomarker in my sample?" I asked.

"We'll take it back to the habitat and run the sample in the wet chemistry lab," Vanessa explained. Then she turned around and helped Pia pull from the trailer a tall wardrobe box holding the prototype astronaut suits.

"When do we leave?" Claire grumbled, and I just sighed, tired of all her grouchiness.

The scientists got to work, rushing around and setting up their delicate instruments. I stayed out of the way and helped myself to a cold water from the cooler bag. Rick took the chains off the rover, and it rolled backward onto the desert sand.

"Cool," I said.

Claire moved her chair farther away from me. "You think everything is so cool and amazing." She crossed her arms and dug deeper into her seat. "It's annoying."

A ball of anger clumped in my throat because she was the one being annoying. Just because she was mad at her dad for the geyser thing didn't mean she could take it out on me. How did I ever think a friendship would work with Claire Jacobs anyway?

I sipped my water, letting the iciness calm me. "I'm not annoyed," I said.

"Whatever," she replied. "You don't even—"

But I cut her off, turning my back to her.

I watched the scientists do their work, sweat dribbling down my back in the heat of the desert even though I was under the shade of the canopy. Pia and Vanessa were in their astronaut suits already, tinkering with a massive drill they had attached to the rover. As I watched them, it was easy to imagine that we were the first humans on the surface of Mars, on the verge of a major discovery.

"Coordinates?" Rick called from his own little tent where he'd set up a workstation. He would run the rover from his laptop.

"24.0793S, 69.7905W," Vanessa said, looking at her notebook.

They were planning to drill several feet into the rocky, dusty floor of the desert, hoping to find evidence of life there, where it was safe from the harsh sun.

"Okay, we're ready," Pia said, standing up from the drill.

Rick started the rover's program, the robot coming to life and rolling calmly across the desert. When it stopped at the right coordinates, the drill started spinning slow and steady and then lowered toward the rocky earth. The scientists stepped under the canopy as the drill slowly plowed its way into the rocky earth.

"I bet nobody else in your school went to the driest place on Earth for winter break," Pia said, her voice muffled behind her astronaut helmet.

"You're right about that!" I said, coughing from the dust that was floating off the scientists' suits. Claire remained quiet, but I couldn't help but notice that her eyes were wide as she watched the drill.

Once it reached its target, the rover slowly brought the drill out of the ground, and the scientists walked over to inspect the work. And then Pia and Vanessa took samples of the dirt from the drill, taking such a long time labeling plastic tubes that I thought for sure they had forgotten their promise to me.

But then, just when I thought I couldn't take the dust and heat and not having anyone to talk to anymore, Pia walked up and asked if I was ready.

"To sample?" I jumped up. "Now? Me?" I looked at Vanessa standing over by the rover and she waved.

"Claire? Do you want to sample too?" Pia asked. She opened up the wardrobe box that had been wheeled into the shade of our tent. "We have a few extra proto-type suits," she said. "These two look pretty small."

I stopped breathing for a second. I was actually standing in front of a NASA scientist wearing a space suit on an official mission.

"Nope." Claire looked away from us, folding her arms.

I flapped my hands to my side in frustration. How could she pass up this kind of opportunity?

Pia waved me off and pulled out a suit. "*Está bien*," she said to me. It's okay. "Leave her be."

"She won't even talk to me," I said, in Spanish so that Claire wouldn't understand. "I thought we could be friends."

"Do not give up so fast," Pia said. "Sometimes being a friend is not about talking. It's about listening." She held out a fabric bodysuit that looked like the long underwear I wear in the winter. It wasn't the kind of outfit I'd want to put on in a super-hot and dry desert.

But I pulled on the suit without complaint, wiping sweat from my forehead.

"One more layer," Pia said, holding the upper torso assembly over my head and I wiggled in, arms first, my head popping out the neckhole. And then she helped me step into the lower torso assembly, some boots and a pair of gloves, snapping and sealing the assembly together.

I glanced at Claire again and shook my head. "I feel like all I do is listen to her complaining, and plus, she can be really mean," I told Pia, my hands getting sweaty in the gloves.

"Make sure you listen with your best ears," Pia said, helping me put on a backpack with a bunch of dials and hoses.

How do I do listen with my best ears? I wondered.

The heat was getting unbearable. I was about to say something when Pia flipped a switch on the pack, and I felt coolness flowing through my bodysuit. Instant relief.

"Ready for your helmet?" Pia asked.

I grinned, giving her a thumbs-up.

She pulled an astronaut helmet out of a wardrobe box and lowered it over my head. "All right, then, come on, Luci," Pia said, and I followed her out into the sun.

I kneeled in the dirt next to Vanessa, feeling a chill of excitement. Pia kneeled on my other side and unwrapped one of the sterilized spatulas on the towel next to her, and Vanessa handed me a tube and a permanent marker. I labeled my tube, "Luciana," my full name because it felt more official.

And then Vanessa showed me how to scoop a sample of dirt from the drill and carefully place it into a tube. I took a long time choosing where to sample my dirt and I finally decided to take a tiny scoop from the very end of the drill where the rover reached down to the deepest and darkest spot. I tapped the dirt from the spatula into the tube and quickly clicked on the top to avoid any contamination. Then I handed the tube to Vanessa, and before she put it in the cooler beside her with the rest of the samples, she smiled at me and wrote something else on my tube.

"Luciana: Future First Girl to Mars."

And even though being the first girl to Mars had been my dream for most of my life, it never felt more real than it did at that moment.

Chapter 10
DAMAGE

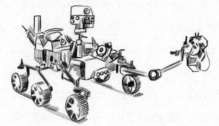

The ride back to the Mars habitat was quiet. The small cooler of samples sat snugly between Claire and me and we used it as an armrest, neither of us letting our elbows touch. We were all sweaty and hungry, and I swore I had dust in my mouth. When we finally arrived at the habitat, Rick instructed us to stay inside until he was done unloading the rover. Claire and I scrambled out of the jeep and raced to the bathroom. I let her go first because it was the nice thing to do even though I had to go so bad it was nearly an emergency.

After I was finished, I rushed back to the airlock to see if Vanessa and Pia needed any help emptying the jeep. From the ramp, I could hear them in the lab tent, chatting as they got their tools ready to test the samples. The jeep's back door was open, and I spotted the cooler in the seat where Claire and I had been sitting. I was so excited for the scientists to start testing the samples—my sample in particular—that I ran out and grabbed the cooler from the back seat. As I made my way around the back of the jeep toward the lab tent, I heard a mechanical noise, like a latch being released.

All of a sudden, Rick called out to me, "Watch out, Luci!"

I looked up and saw the rover rolling backward off the trailer—and heading straight toward me!

"Luci! Get out of the way!" Rick shouted. "Now!"

Panicked, I sprinted out of the way, the cooler slipping out of my hand. Immediately, I turned around to try to retrieve it, but Rick grabbed me around the waist.

"What were you thinking?" Rick asked, his eyes bulging, his face red.

"I—I was—" I started.

"I told you to stay inside until I finished unloading the rover," he scolded. "What were you doing out here? You could have been seriously injured."

"I wasn't thinking," I said. "I was just so excited to test the samples that I . . ." My voice trembled and I trailed off.

Rick took a deep breath and asked, "Are you hurt?"

I shook my head. By now, Pia, Vanessa, and Claire had come to see what the commotion was all about. My face blazed like it was on fire, partially from the hot sun, but mostly from complete and total humiliation. I had basically walked right in front of the rover.

Rick brushed the hair out of his face, pacing. "That was too close. Way too close. We're so lucky you're okay."

And that's when I saw the true damage. The cooler was cracked and smashed to pieces, run over by the one-thousand-pound rover.

"The samples!" Vanessa cried. She kneeled in front of the cooler, pulling a splintered piece of the handle out from under a tire.

I felt dizzy, because if the samples were crushed too, they would be contaminated and useless.

"Are the samples okay?" I asked.

Why did I think I should be the one to bring the cooler to the lab? I had acted without thinking—again. When I was at Space Camp, I accused another robotics team of cheating without having any evidence. Not only did I nearly ruin the competition for that team, I almost got my own team sent home as well. Once again, my thoughtlessness had ruined everything.

The rest of the astronauts gathered around Vanessa, and as each of their faces changed from hopeful to serious, I knew the samples were toast.

Claire looked at me and shrugged. I couldn't tell if her shrug was the mean kind of shrug like "too-bad-so-sad" or a kind of friendly sympathy shrug.

"I'm so sorry," I said again, staring at my shoes. "This is all my fault."

"Don't be sorry," Vanessa said. "It was an accident. Accidents happen all the time in science. Although you really shouldn't have come outside while Rick was unchaining the rover," she added.

"I wasn't thinking," I tried to explain again. But I knew my excuses were useless. The scientists' final mission had been ruined. And it was all my fault.

I peered around the scientists' huddle to see the damage for myself. The tubes were cracked and the samples had spilled. I wanted to crawl under a rock somewhere and cry.

Claire's phone rang from inside. She tore back into the habitat, leaving me there alone with the scientists, pretending I got dust in my eye as they discussed what to do now.

The scientists figured out pretty quickly that they

had to go back to the site. They'd camp there overnight so they could take their samples first thing in the morning. It was the only option since they needed those samples for the university and they had to be back in time to catch their flight to the United States, which was leaving tomorrow.

I went inside, plopped down on a chair at the dining table, and watched the scientists organize and clean up their workstations, not daring to ask if they needed my help.

"Claire, was that your dad calling?" Vanessa asked, pushing a jacket into her backpack.

Claire looked up from the snack she made at the counter. "Yep. He was all ready to fly back, but his pilot had to run out to get a part for the helicopter. So once the helicopter is ready, they'll take off. It won't be long."

"Unfortunately, we need to get going right away so we can set up camp before sunset," Rick said. "So we'll have to leave you two here until Claire's dad gets back."

I nodded, knowing there was nothing more to say.

Vanessa deposited a stack of logbooks into a box. "You two will be fine here, though, right?"

"Sure, yeah," Claire said.

I nodded, but was worried. Would I be left here with the nice Claire or the not-so-friendly one?

And then I was swamped with guilt and embarrassment on top of worry because they wouldn't be leaving me with Claire in the first place if it hadn't been for my huge mistake. Even though they were trying to be nice about it, I knew I cost them an entire day of work and maybe even a lot of money.

"I'll call my dad if we need anything. He'll be back before we know it," Claire said.

"Okay," Vanessa said. "We'll have our satellite phones with us if you need anything." And then she walked away with her box of stuff.

I looked at Claire, but didn't know what to say to her. I felt like I should apologize, but for what? Before I could say anything, she rolled her eyes and disappeared up the ladder to the next floor.

The scientists were almost ready to go. I stayed out of the way and watched as they finished packing, pulled food out of the fridge for the night, cleaned up the galley, and brought their bags down from their crew quarters.

Pia stopped at the dining table, where I was sitting. She juggled a heavy bag on one shoulder and a giant laptop in her arms. "Hey, sorry about taking off like this."

I felt my eyes well up again, but I managed to pull myself together. "I'm really sorry. Like so, so—"

She stopped me. "You're not the first person on this team to make a mistake," she said in Spanish. "In fact, on my first mission out here, I left our entire tool bag at the sampling site and halfway home we had to turn around and drive back."

"But what I did was much worse," I said.

"Luci, I know you will learn to think with your *cabeza*," she said, pointing to my head. "Even though I know sometimes it's easier to think with your *corazón* instead," pointing to her heart. "You just have to slow down sometimes, have a little patience."

I nodded, taking in Pia's advice.

"Anyway, don't let one flub make you doubt yourself," Pia continued. "Perfection is overrated, and learning from your mistakes will only make you a stronger future astronaut."

"Pia, we're ready!" Rick called from the airlock.

"On my way," she said, and then she gave me a big hug. "I know I'll see you around someday, Luci. Good luck. Have faith in yourself. Keep in touch." And then she yelled, *"Adiós,* Claire!" up the ladder before spinning toward the airlock, and then heading outside.

I heard the jeep rumble to a start, and when I looked out the window, I saw the rover safely tethered to its trailer again.

They beeped as they drove away, and I watched them bump along the desert until they disappeared over a hill.

Chapter 11

TIGHT SPACES

I climbed the ladder and found Claire in our pod, on the top bunk, earplugs in, listening to something on her phone. I rooted around in my bag for the tin full of Abuelita's pan de Pascua, and pulled out two slices of Christmas bread loaded with candied fruit and nuts. I stood up and waved a piece in front of her, hoping she might accept the peace offering and let go of whatever grudge she was holding against me. Instead, she snatched it up and then lay back down. No thanks or anything.

Frustrated, I climbed into my lower bunk to eat my bread. Papa's toy car was next to my pillow. I tucked it in closer to me as I got comfortable, grateful that Abuelita had thought to give me the car and the bread for this trip. It was as if she knew I would need it. *I'll be home tomorrow,* I told myself. But where would Abuelita's home be when I returned?

My mind cycled through everything that had gone wrong since I arrived in Chile—my failed reunion with my cousins, the earthquake and Abuelita's damaged house, my broken friendship with Claire, our sampling mission in the desert. As I let the hopelessness wash over me, a tear slid down my cheek.

All of a sudden, the bunk bed shifted.

"Claire?" I called, and the bed shifted again but this time I realized the entire pod was shaking.

As the room shook violently around us, I realized this was nothing like the shaking I had felt at Abuelita's house.

This was the big one. The terremoto.

"Luci!" I heard Claire call.

The entire habitat rocked back and forth, and my body slammed against the wall—*bam! bam!*—again and again. Desperately, I grabbed the side of the bed, praying that the horrible shaking would stop.

Suddenly, my bed collapsed, slamming down hard on the ground. One of the bunk bed support beams sliced through the air, hitting my arm before slamming onto the mattress next to me. And then I heard Claire scream as her top bunk came crashing down. I braced myself for the impact, squeezing my eyes closed. But when I felt no pain, I opened my eyes again and realized I was trapped in a narrow pocket between the two beds.

And then just like at Abuelita's house, the jerking stopped and I was left there on my bed, my heartbeat pounding through my entire body. My arm throbbed with pain. Everything was dark, the top bunk cutting off my view of the cupola with its seven windows looking out to the stars.

"Claire?" I called. I tried to pull my throbbing arm toward my body, but couldn't move in the tiny space between the beds. "Claire! I'm stuck!" I didn't hear anything. What if the beds shifted some more and squashed me as flat as the cooler? What if Claire was hurt?

My brain flooded with the same panic I'd felt when I was stuck in the underwater closet.

What if Claire had left me—again?

Then I heard Claire's muffled voice. "Luci?"

There was rustling around from above, and I felt the top bed frame push closer to me, pinning me against the wall. I screamed.

"Luci!" There was panic in Claire's voice then. "Luci, are you hurt?"

"I'm stuck, Claire. Help me!" Fear swelled in my body. "Please don't leave!"

"I'm here, Luci," she called to me. "I can get you out. Trust me."

I was sobbing now. My heart was beating too fast and I couldn't calm myself down. How many people died of heart attacks while waiting to be rescued after an earthquake?

"Claire!" I called again. "Claire!"

"It's okay. I'm here." Claire's voice was clear and calm. "Take a breath. Are you hurt?"

"I think so," I sobbed, feeling waves of pain in my arm. But being trapped felt worse than the pain. I tried to control my breathing, but the terror pulsing through my body was too great to ignore. I started to hyperventilate. "I . . . have to . . . get . . . out of here!" I wailed between breaths.

"Okay," she said. "But first you need to slow down your breathing. Tell me what you see."

She was using her trick to try to calm me down. But it wasn't going to work. No way. Not this time. I gulped for air.

"Tell me what you see," she said again. "Luci? You can do this."

"Nothing!" I yelled. "Nothing but blackness!"

"Okay, then, what do you smell?" she said, and actually I smelled a lot. Like, dirt and laundry soap and ink and Abuelita's Christmas bread. As I listed those smells, I started to slow my breathing down. I wanted to wipe my nose, but I was so wedged against the wall, I couldn't move my hand.

I felt something shift. Dread swept over my body. Was it an aftershock? I screamed again.

"That was me," Claire called. "I moved the bed a little. See if you can shimmy out."

"What?" I said. "No, I can't. I'm totally stuck in here, Claire."

"Luci, you have to try," Claire urged. "You have to get out of there. I'm worried the bed frame could fall all the way on top of you."

I squirmed a bit, but every time I heard the bed shift, I became paralyzed by panic. There was no way I could squeeze out from the small space without sending the top bunk slamming down onto me.

"Just do it, Luci!" Claire said, practically yelling.

I bit my lip to try to stop myself from crying and worked harder to move down the bed. And what if there *was* an aftershock? Then I'd have to wait in this coffin until Mr. Jacobs got here, whenever that would be, and probably I'd die from a heart attack by that time.

"Keep doing what you're doing. I see your foot," Claire said. "There's an opening here. You just have to squeeze yourself through."

I took a slow breath. There were no other options. I had to get free before the bed fell all the way.

I couldn't move my arms, so I dug my heels into the bed, and scooched down, inch by inch. "You're doing great," Claire said. "Your foot is out now." I felt her hand on my foot.

Claire pulled my leg while I shimmied, and we were making great progress until one of my shoulders hit a bar that I couldn't wedge myself past.

"Why'd you stop? You're halfway out," Claire said, but she sounded different somehow, almost like her words were thicker and running together. Or was it me? Was my air being cut off? Was I losing consciousness?

"There's a bar," I said. "I can't get my shoulder through." But Claire didn't give up, and she pulled harder on my leg. Finally, my shoulder popped free, and a sharp pain streaked down the entire length of my body. I tumbled onto the floor.

That's when I saw Claire. Her head was bleeding. She teetered and collapsed on top of me.

"Claire! Claire!" I shouted. But she didn't move.

I was okay, but clearly Claire wasn't.

CHAPTER 12
THE BIG ONE

Claire's eyes flickered open and she mumbled something I couldn't understand. I carefully nudged her off me and then helped her sit up on the floor. I grabbed a sheet from her bed and wiped the blood off her face and neck. Once she was cleaned up a bit, I could see that the blood was coming from a head wound. I carefully dabbed at the cut, ignoring my own fears that I wouldn't be able to save Claire after she saved me. I knew that head wounds bled a lot. When my best friend from home, Raelyn, knocked her head into one of her kitchen cabinets, a tiny cut on her forehead had made a huge mess of her new shirt. But Claire's injury looked more serious than Rae's, and I worried that Claire also had a concussion.

Claire tried to touch her head, and I swatted her hand away. "We need to get the first aid kit. Can you walk?"

She slowly nodded her head, and I helped her stand.

Then, with my good arm supporting her, I helped her climb down the ladder. We tread carefully past the overturned workstations and the shattered computer monitor, all the time looking at each other like neither of us could believe we were here. Alone. During an emergency.

"You're bleeding, Luci," she said, pointing to my arm.

I tried moving my arm. Between getting hit with the support beam when the bunk collapsed and having to scrape past the pole, my arm was definitely bruised up and bleeding a bit, but, as far as I could tell, it wasn't broken. I knew that Claire was more injured than me.

"Don't worry about me, Claire," I said. "Let's take care of you first."

The lights in the habitat flickered on and off. We held on to each other as we walked, not able to see what was broken on the floor beneath us.

"First we have to get the flashlight," I told Claire. "Pia said it was in the bench in the airlock."

I started walking, but Claire froze. "Do you hear that? Do you think it's a helicopter?"

I paused and shook my head. No helicopter. But I did hear a beeping noise, like an alarm or a telephone ring. The satellite phone!

"I think the scientists are trying to reach us!" I shouted.

"Maybe they have news about my dad," Claire said.

Desperately, I searched through the mess for the satellite phone. At last, I found it under a pile of collapsed shelves.

I pressed a button and said, "This is Luci. Can you hear me?"

There was a short pause and then: "Yes, Luci, we hear you! This is Vanessa. Are you girls okay?"

I looked at Claire's forehead and saw that it was shiny in the dark. Glistening. "Claire has a cut on her head, and my arm hurts, but basically we're okay. The habitat's a wreck, though." Another pause. It sounded like the connection was going in and out. "Vanessa? Are you still there? Are you okay?"

"I'm still here," Vanessa reported, "and we're safe. The jeep sustained some damage, but we should be able to fix it by the morning. I'm worried about you girls, though," Vanessa continued. We had to strain to hear her as the connection began to break up. "We hope to be back to the habitat early tomorrow. Girls, I think we're about to lose the satellite—"

Claire grabbed the satellite phone from my hand.

"Have you heard anything from my dad?" she asked. It was like Claire held her breath waiting for Vanessa's answer.

There was no response.

"Vanessa?" Claire cried. "Can you hear me?" But we had lost contact with the scientists.

"My phone is upstairs. I need to call my dad," Claire cried. "Like, now."

"Claire," I said, trying to hold on to her. "Let's take care of the cut on your head and then we can try him on the satellite phone once we make a connection again. Okay?"

Claire wiped a tear from her eye and nodded.

Shuffling together in the flickering light, we crossed the threshold into the airlock. I lunged for the storage bench, pushing aside blankets and paper suits in plastic wrap. Finally, I found a flashlight under a bag of tools.

I picked up a blanket and put it around Claire's shoulders, trying not to get any blood on it, which was pointless anyway. "I remember Pia telling us there's a first aid kit in the hygiene module," I told her. "You stay here while I go find it. Okay?"

Claire nodded and sat down on the storage bench.

I tracked back over to the main area, through the galley, and past the communications table where drawers had fallen open and spilled out their contents. I stepped over pens and pencils and sampling spatulas in sterile wrapping and timers and broken glassware until I reached the hygiene module.

Then the habitat went dark.

"You okay?" I yelled back to Claire through the habitat. When I didn't get an answer, I found the storage cabinet with my flashlight and tore through it, searching frantically for the extra first aid kit. I finally found it stuffed in the back corner behind the toilet paper. "Got it!" I called. "I'm coming, Claire!"

I raced back through the main core of the habitat to Claire, hoping she hadn't lost consciousness again.

But when I got back to the airlock, I stopped short, dropping the first aid kit at my feet. Gauze and tape and bandages rolled across the floor. Claire wasn't passed out on the storage bench as I had feared.

She was gone. And the door to the outside was flung open and banging against the wall in the desert wind.

CHAPTER 13

ABANDONED

I grabbed a handful of gauze and the roll of tape, leaving the rest of the mess on the floor, and ran outside. The desert wind had turned frigid, and I rubbed my bare arms against the cold. As I pounded down the ramp and past the outdoor lab, a sharp odor prickled my nose. It smelled dangerous, like gasoline, and made my eyes water. I wanted to investigate, but first I needed to find Claire. That's when I spotted the white blanket that I had given Claire on the ground in front of me, flapping in the wind, like a broken bird. Abandoned, just as I had been.

"Claire!" I turned on my flashlight and flashed it around the desert. "Claire!"

She was gone.

Panic formed a lump in my throat, and my eyes filled with tears. I was angry at Claire for leaving me and afraid that she was hurt and needed my help.

Where did she go? She couldn't have gone off to look for her dad. We would have heard his helicopter, and he was too far away to reach by foot. But what if the earthquake reached as far as Antofagasta? My heart clenched, and my mind was spinning out of control. What about Santiago? Had the earthquake hit there too? *Please, not Santiago,* I thought. *Please let my family be safe.*

I forced myself to take a breath and closed my eyes for a second. I needed to calm down. Right now I had to focus on finding Claire. I couldn't let her stumble around a dark desert, injured and not thinking straight.

I heard a clicking noise. "Claire?" I called again, but as I came around the side of the hygiene module, I realized the noise was coming from the generator, a machine that powered the habitat and gave it electricity. It was lying on its side in a pool of diesel fuel, which trickled under the habitat. I tried pulling the generator upright to stop the leak, but pain shot through my arm and I dropped the heavy machine back onto the ground.

"Claire!" I called again.

I shined my flashlight on the rocky ground and took a few steps into the desert. I didn't want to go too far, fearing that I would lose sight of the darkened habitat.

The desert had a way of swallowing up everything in its blackness. Kind of like outer space, I imagined.

"Claire!" My body flooded with anger at her selfishness. It's not like we didn't have enough to worry about with her head injury, a generator gushing flammable fuel under our only shelter, and—

Then out of the corner of my eye I saw some movement. I whipped my head around and was able to make out Claire's faint silhouette, on top of a rock formation that rose from the sand like a small mountain.

I ran toward her, afraid she would flee from me and stumble deeper into danger. Afraid there'd be another tremor and she'd fall off the mountain.

I pointed the flashlight down, leaping over sharp rocks and cracks in the ground that might have been caused by the earthquake. I climbed up the steep hill on my hands and knees, ignoring the pain in my injured arm. "Claire," I said, staggering over to her.

She turned around. "He's not coming."

"What?"

"My dad. I would see the helicopter's lights from up here, or hear the beating of the rotors. Helicopters are super loud."

I handed her the wad of gauze. "Put this on your head, Claire. And of course he's coming. He's probably stuck in Antofagasta."

"Or crashed somewhere and maybe needs help," she said.

"We can't worry about that right now. Why did you run out here all by yourself?" I was yelling now, while at the same time trying to bite off a piece of medical tape to hold the gauze down. "I was getting you a first aid kit. What if you have a concussion? And what if we can't—" I stopped, turning around, looking for the white reflection of the habitat, but I couldn't see it anymore. "What if we can't find our way back?" When she didn't answer, I continued yelling. "We're all alone out here and we need to be a team. Haven't you learned yet that you don't abandon your partner?"

Claire looked at me in quiet shock, because she knew that I wasn't just talking about right now in the desert. She knew I was talking about the time we were partners in the pool too. And as often as we'd been messaging, we had never talked about what happened since she apologized at the end of camp.

I knew it was a bad time to bring that up, but it just came out.

My parents were right: I was still angry at Claire for what happened. And even though I had accepted her apology, it was obvious to me now that I was far from forgiving her. Maybe some people didn't deserve a second chance after all.

"I didn't abandon you again," she said. "I was just looking for my dad's helicopter."

How did she not see that running out into the desert was abandoning me, that what she did put both of us in danger?

"Leaving someone in the middle of a crisis situation is the exact definition of abandoning," I said. I knew this kind of Claire. The kind that only thought of herself. The Claire that I couldn't trust.

She didn't say anything and that was all I needed, for Claire to go silent on me again. I sighed. "Forget it."

She stood up and she must have dislodged a small rock because I heard it clatter down the hill. Then Claire reached down and picked up another rock, throwing it this time.

"I mean, if someone ever left me in a pool like that, I wouldn't forgive them either," Claire said, throwing another rock. It took a while to land, but with nothing but silence around us, we eventually heard it hit the ground somewhere in the distance. "Is that why you kept telling me not to leave when you were stuck under the bunk bed?"

I nodded, picking up my own rock, but when I held it in my hand, it turned to dust and blew away.

"You don't trust me," she said, tossing another rock. "I guess I wouldn't trust me either."

"Claire—" I started, but she cut me off.

"What's that?" She pointed out into the desert, her voice urgent.

I looked over my shoulder and at first I didn't see anything, but then a tiny orange flicker came into focus.

"Is that a fire?" she asked. She dropped the rest of the rocks from her hand.

"Claire," I said. "I think it's the habitat."

And then I remembered the overturned generator, and the pool of fuel trickling under the habitat.

I grabbed Claire's hand, and we raced down the hill. We had to put out the fire and save the habitat. Otherwise, we might not survive the night.

CHAPTER 14

TEAM OF TWO

We half slid and half ran back to the habitat, the rocky terrain slowing us down as the flame expanded from a small spark to a glowing blaze.

As we got closer, I could see that the fire was in the lab tent, just feet away from the overturned generator. If we didn't contain the fire in time, the entire habitat would go up in flames.

"We have to move faster," I shouted, pulling Claire along.

The door to the airlock had slammed shut in the wind and I tore it open, handing Claire my flashlight and grabbing the fire extinguisher from the storage bench.

"Luci!" Claire shrieked.

When I turned back around, I saw that the fire had spread to the tent fabric, climbing fast, and for a moment

I was frozen in fear. What if the lab chemicals exploded? Or let out dangerous gases?

"Luci! Go!" Claire said, snapping me back to reality. For a fleeting second we made eye contact and I knew how much we were counting on each other to make it through this disaster. Claire could absolutely count on me, but—my heart skipped a beat—could I count on her?

I ran back to the tent, pulled the pin on the extinguisher, aimed, and fired the powdery foam at the flames. It came out fast, some of it catching in the wind, getting in my hair and eyes and mouth. I stepped closer to the tent and I could feel the waves of heat on my skin and the choke of smoke in my lungs. But I held my ground until every single flame was out, spraying and spraying until there was no more to spray.

And too late I realized that there was one spark that had escaped, an ember dancing in the wind, dipping up and down in the already ravaged chemical tent.

"Claire!" I called. "Go see if there's another fire extinguisher!" But she just stood there, watching me, in a stunned and scared kind of way. "Look in the galley, Claire!" I glanced over my shoulder and saw Claire running away from the lab tent, in the opposite direction of the habitat.

She was racing into the desert with my flashlight.

"Claire! DON'T LEAVE!" My eyes flooded with tears because I couldn't do this alone. I needed help. I was counting on her. "Claire!"

And then the ember landed and I saw a line of fire zipping over the trail of diesel fuel, straight for the puddle beneath the habitat. I knew there was nothing left for me to do. I ran for safety, expecting to hear an explosion.

Out of the corner of my eye, I saw a flash of light and it took me a second to realize that it was Claire with the flashlight. She was running past me with the white blanket that she had discarded in the desert, and before I could figure out what she was doing, she threw the blanket onto the flames near the habitat.

"No! Claire!" I yelled, because she wasn't thinking straight. She was going to get burned.

But then, in one swoop, the flames were gone.

I exhaled, all at once realizing I had been holding my breath.

"Fire blanket," Claire called out to me.

"What?" I said, walking over to her, still trying to catch my breath. "How did you know that?"

She pointed to a little embroidered flame sewn onto the tag. "My dad has one in his lab."

Claire hadn't left me. She had saved us.

I picked up the flashlight Claire had dropped and we stood together, breathing heavily and shivering in the desert wind.

Claire lifted the blanket. "It's out."

We walked through the lab tent, checking to make sure that nothing else was smoldering and could rekindle a fire. We found a small cabinet that said "FLAMMABLE LIQUID." It was open and on its side, a shattered bottle on the ground next to it. "Must have been a chemical fire," I said.

We secured the rest of the chemicals so that if there was a strong aftershock, no more bottles would break. Then I walked Claire around the habitat and stood in front of the generator.

"It's leaking fuel," I explained. "Even though we've put out the flames, it's still too dangerous to have fuel leaking under the habitat. And I don't know about you, but I'm getting cold out here. If we want to spend the night in the habitat, we need to be able to go back inside without the threat of another fire. I think we can lift it if we try together," I said.

Claire agreed. "I'll pull and you push," she said.

We positioned ourselves on either side of the

generator. It was framed in a metal cage, which gave us a good handle to try to lift it.

"Ready?" Claire asked, her back to the moon, making her look like a ghostly silhouette. "One . . . two . . . three!"

We heaved, but couldn't get enough leverage to tilt it onto its end.

"This time, we try harder," I said, though my arm was already throbbing from the effort, and I worried this would be too much for Claire. I looked her in the eye. "Ready?"

"Ready," she said, leaning over. The smell of diesel fuel made us both cough.

"Go!" Claire yelled, and together, we pushed and pulled one more time.

And with a thud and a splash of fuel, the generator was right side up again.

CHAPTER 15

A LONG NIGHT

We waited outside until all of the fuel seeped into the desert sand. I kept checking over my shoulder, half expecting to see more flames in the chemistry lab, feeling relieved when all I saw was charred debris and what was left of the tent.

"Whoa," Claire said when we went back into the airlock. "We don't smell so good."

It was true. We smelled like we took a shower in gasoline, but neither of us had the energy to climb the ladder up to our pod to look for new clothes. My bag was most certainly beneath the collapsed bunk bed and out of reach anyway. Along with Papa's toy car, I realized with a pang of regret. How did I let Papa's car get away when I needed it now more than ever? It was the last connection I had to my family out here in the desert. What if . . .

I pushed all the bad thoughts from my mind and focused on helping Claire.

"We should clean that up better," I said, pointing to her head wound.

I picked up a bunch of wet wipe packets and some fresh gauze and tape from the floor, and Claire sat down on the storage bench. Her teeth chattered even though we were inside. The airlock provided little warmth.

"Tell me if I hurt you, okay?" I said, peeling open the first packet of antibacterial wipes.

"I probably won't feel anything. I'm so worried," she said. "I can't stop thinking about my dad."

I dabbed the side of her face, and for a second, I felt woozy at the sight of her injury.

Claire hissed through her teeth, pulling away from me as I covered her cut with fresh gauze. After I finished bandaging her wound, I smeared some antibacterial cream on my own cut and covered it up with a bandage, a sharp pain making my eyes water every time I moved my arm.

"I think we should try to sleep in here tonight," I said, looking around the airlock. "We'll be able to make a quick escape if anything goes wrong."

Claire nodded. "We'll need these," she said, pulling a stack of blankets out of the storage bench.

We layered the blankets on the floor, making two beds. And then we sat in our separate little nests, the flashlight between us, standing on its end and pointing to the ceiling.

After a few minutes, Claire broke the silence. "I'm scared," she said.

"Me too," I said, letting my thoughts flood back in. Even though the earthquake was scary and the fires were terrifying, the kind of scared I felt now was even worse. It was as if I had used up all my bravery escaping from small spaces and chasing Claire into the desert and fighting fires. Now the fear of not getting rescued prickled up, and I had no courage left to fight it.

I peered at the satellite phone. "NO SERVICE."

"I don't think I'll be able to sleep for a while," I said.

She shook her head. "Me neither." Then she got on her knees and started riffling through the storage bench again. "Hey, what's this?" she asked, pulling out a device that looked like a flashlight with dials and buttons.

"It's a radio!" I said, taking it from her. "The hand-crank kind. My dad has an old one of these at home for emergencies." I pulled out the crank and wound it up. No batteries were needed for this kind of radio.

I put the radio on the floor, cranking and cranking, and Claire pulled out the antenna and pushed the power button. *BEEP BEEP BEEP*. And then there was a man speaking in Spanish.

Claire looked at me. "What's he saying?"

"He's saying the epicenter of the earthquake hit thirty kilometers off the coast of Antofagasta."

Claire sucked in a breath.

"Magnitude 8.8."

We stared at each other in silence, both of us realizing just how big the earthquake had really been. The highest you could go was a magnitude ten.

"Widespread damage . . . oh, he's talking about tsunamis now." I listened. "Waves are five meters high . . . boats pushed onto land . . . seek higher ground . . ." I stopped translating, seeing Claire's face go slack. The news was all of her worst nightmares combined. The earthquake had been the most severe in Antofagasta, and on top of everything, there was now the threat of tsunamis.

"The airstrip is by the water," Claire said numbly.

"Maybe your dad wasn't." But then, what about his helicopter sitting on the airstrip? Had it been damaged in the earthquake?

"I didn't even say good-bye to him this morning," Claire said. "I was so mad at him for leaving me."

I wrapped myself in a blanket, the chill of the airlock working its way through my clothes.

"I forgot to tell you what your dad said when he left," I said. Claire looked up. "He wanted me to tell you he loves you."

"He always says that when he's leaving." She sniffed. "I don't usually get so angry, it's just"—she took a breath—"he missed my chorus concert last week because something came up and he promised he'd be there." She glanced at me. "Not that chorus is that important." She shrugged.

"Chorus concerts are important," I said. "I get that."

"I know he does important work and I know that sometimes he can't be around. But . . ." A tear dripped down her face and she wiped it away.

"But what?"

"Sometimes a kid just needs her dad, you know?" She pulled a blanket over her bent knees and up to her chin.

"Yeah," I said.

"It would be nice if he needed me too," Claire added quietly. "Sometimes I think he should just send me to a boarding school or something. Then he could travel anywhere without worrying about me or feeling bad for leaving me behind." She took a shuddery breath. "I even found one that has a really good science program. I know he'll like it. He'd probably sign me up in a heartbeat." She wiped her nose. "I already filled out the application."

"Claire . . ." I said.

She shook her head. "Don't feel sad for me. My life isn't that hard. And I'd go to that science school without a complaint if it meant he was safe right now." She sniffed.

I shifted my blanket-bed closer to hers. "I didn't know you were thinking about all this."

"You never asked." She picked at a fuzz on her blanket.

At first I felt stung by Claire's words. But then I realized that Pia was right: I hadn't been listening with my best ears. I could have been a better friend to Claire all this time if only I had slowed down and given her a chance to talk. If I had listened more. If I had asked what was really bothering her.

Claire cranked the radio, turning the broadcast back on.

And as I sat there in my little makeshift bed, half listening to the radio, something suddenly flicked on in my brain. Had I made the same mistake with my cousins that I had with Claire? Had I been doing all the talking? I was so sure that by telling them about my adventures and making them proud that they'd want me to be the fifth member of Los Cuatro. Had I even once asked them about what they were doing? Or about their school? Or about their adventures? How did I not even know that Julieta was a photographer?

And the answer burned my stomach. It was because I had never asked.

Claire and I took turns cranking the radio and after a while I said, "Tsunami warning was lifted."

"Good," Claire said, her voice only a whisper. "Did they say if anyone was really hurt or anything?"

"No," I said, even though I had heard the announcer say there were several missing people. I closed my eyes, wishing and wishing and wishing one of those people wasn't Mr. Jacobs.

"Hey, Claire?" I said. "I could have been more

understanding, you know, when your dad had to go to his meeting. You were really upset that he forgot all about your plans, and I should have been nicer to you."

Claire looked at the ground. "It wasn't your problem."

"It should have been, though," I said. "If I had been a better friend."

"I should be the one apologizing." She cranked the radio. "I didn't mean to abandon you. Again."

I sighed, shimmying under my covers. "I should have told you I was still mad about what happened at the pool. That I hadn't really forgiven you all the way."

Claire snorted. "I haven't forgiven myself either. So, we're even I guess."

"My mom said"—my heart panged at the thought of my mom—"that it's pretty hard to have a friendship without forgiveness."

"Your mom sounds pretty smart," Claire said.

"Well, maybe we should both forgive so we can start being real friends?" I asked.

Claire pulled her blanket down. "Do you think you can really forgive me this time?"

She had left me in the pool, and that was really dangerous, but today she stayed by my side when my life was in danger. Not only did she pull me out of the bunk bed when she was dealing with her own injuries, but she also risked her life when she put out the fire. And I felt like if I needed her to be there for me again, I could trust that she would be.

"Yes," I said. And I meant it for real this time.

Claire smiled at me. Then she yawned and sank lower into her bed. Eventually we stopped cranking the radio, and then the only sound in the still habitat was the wind against its walls. Every so often Claire would lift her head, listening extra hard, and I knew she was hoping to hear an approaching helicopter.

As I lay on my blankets, I worried about the scientists out in the desert. I worried about Mr. Jacobs and his helicopter and getting rescued from this habitat. I worried about how I messed things up with my cousins. I worried about my family worrying about me.

Most of all, I worried about Claire. I knew that after someone got a concussion, you were supposed to wake them up throughout the night. I reached over and grabbed her hand and I was surprised when she held on to it.

"When I squeeze your hand, you squeeze back so I know you're okay, all right?"

"Sure, okay," she said.

And that's how we spent the rest of the night, squeezing each other's hand and waiting for the first signs of sunlight.

CHAPTER 16

REUNIONS

A few hours later, as the sun began to peek out from behind the Atacama mountains, we heard the sound of a helicopter's rotors beating loudly overhead. We flipped off our blankets and raced outside. The helicopter had barely touched down before the passenger door swung open and Mr. Jacobs sprinted across the sand. Claire flew into his arms, and he swung her into the air. She was crying and maybe even Mr. Jacobs was crying, and the entire scene made me tear up too, standing there by myself on the ramp to the Mars habitat, thinking about reuniting with my own family.

When Mr. Jacobs and Claire broke from their hug, Mr. Jacobs spotted the burnt-down chemistry lab. He touched the canvas tent cover, a bit of the charred edge falling off in his hand.

"Oh," Claire said, picking up the empty fire extinguisher. "We had to put out a fire last night."

Mr. Jacobs glanced from Claire to me. "You girls fought a fire with a fire extinguisher last night?"

I nodded, joining them next to the lab tent, my tender arm braced snugly against my stomach.

"And with a fire blanket," Claire added. "Because a puddle of fuel caught fire."

Mr. Jacobs shook his head, like he couldn't believe it. "Wow. Just. Wow." But then he got serious again, squeezing Claire tighter to his side. "I'm so sorry I couldn't be here." He bit his lip, looking away. "I was so worried about you all night." He wiped his eyes. "No more IOUs, Claire. No more. I'm going to cut back on work and spend more time at home."

Claire backed away from him. "No, Dad."

"Honey—" Mr. Jacobs started.

Claire held up her hand. "Listen. I want to go to boarding school."

Mr. Jacobs stood up straighter, surprised. "Where is this coming from?" he asked.

I could see that Claire's chin was trembling. She took a breath and let everything spill out. "I've just been thinking that if I go off to boarding school, then you can work and travel and not worry about me. Because I feel like I'm making it harder for you to do your job. And

I know what you do is really important. You are going to send the first people to Mars someday, and who am I to stand in the way of progress?" A tear slid down her cheek.

"Sweetheart." Mr. Jacobs shook his head. "You're not standing in the way of anything. You're my daughter. I love you. And I don't need to work more, Claire bear. I need more time with my daughter who's growing up too fast."

He needed Claire. I smiled.

"Really?" Claire asked, the pink returning to her face.

Mr. Jacobs hugged her. "I wish it hadn't taken a massive earthquake for you to tell me all this. I can't imagine life without you, Claire. Last night was the longest night of my life not knowing if you were okay."

"Yeah. It was a long night for us too," Claire said. She smiled up at me. "But we were fine, right, Luci?"

"Yeah," I said, meeting her eyes. "More than fine."

Then I heard the satellite phone ring from inside the habitat.

"The scientists!" I said. I ran into the airlock and picked up the satellite phone.

There was a pause and then, *"Hola,* Luci. It's Pia."

"Pia! Mr. Jacobs is here. He's safe. And now so are we!" I shouted.

"That's great news," Pia responded. "I'm so glad you girls are okay."

"And how are you and the rest of the scientists?" I asked.

"We are good. We were able to collect our samples and fix the jeep. In fact, we are just packing up our things and heading back to the habitat," Pia reported.

"What about your flight back to the university?" I asked.

"All flights have been canceled due to the earthquake," Pia said. "Right now, all we can do is go back to the habitat and clean everything up."

"Well, we had a pretty wild night, which I'm sure you'll see when you return to the habitat," I said. "And we will probably be gone by the time you get back, so thanks again—for everything."

"I'm sure I'll be seeing you around, Luci," Pia said.

We said good-bye and hung up. As I put down the satellite phone, I breathed a sigh of relief, thankful the scientists were able to complete their mission, despite the trouble I had caused.

"Are you ready to go back to Santiago?" Mr. Jacobs asked me.

I smiled, but suddenly my heart lurched with dread. What would I be coming home to? Would Abuelita's house be destroyed? "Have you heard any news about Santiago?" I asked Mr. Jacobs. "Do they have any earthquake damage?"

He turned around, a metal box in his hand. "Santiago was far enough from the epicenter of the earthquake to escape damage. In fact, they probably never even felt it. But still, I'm sure your parents are worried sick about you, especially since cell phone service hasn't been restored around here yet." He put his arm around my shoulders. "Let's get you home, Luci."

My eyes welled up just thinking about home. My family. My abuelita and my cousins. Claire patted me on the back, and we walked out of the habitat together, Mr. Jacobs behind us.

Mr. Jacobs used the helicopter pilot's satellite phone to send a message to my parents that I was coming home. We rode in silence for most of the time in the helicopter, all of us looking out the window, watching as we left the desert behind for taller buildings and a view of the Pacific Ocean. We flew back into the Santiago airport and took a car the rest of the way to my family's neighborhood.

When we pulled onto Abuelita's street, Mom, Dad, and Abuelita were watching some of the little cousins play on the playground. The car had barely stopped before I opened the door and tripped outside. Izzy was the first to see me. "Lulu!" she called from the top of a slide.

Everyone turned around, and I barreled toward them, feeling like I hadn't seen them in weeks when it had only been two days. The longest two days of my life.

"*¡Mi niña!*" Abuelita called.

And then it was Mom, Dad, Abuelita, and me in one giant family hug, the little cousins joining us and Izzy pulling my shirt until I picked her up. Aunt Lorena and some of the other aunts and uncles came, hearing the commotion, and even my four cousins stopped what they were doing to run over. It was the best kind of welcome wagon ever.

"Your arm," Mom said, touching my bandage. It didn't hurt as much as it had last night, the pulsing pain now only a dull ache. I looked down at myself and saw what they must have seen. Ripped shorts, streaks of mud and ashes on my skin, my tank top stained with red desert dirt. Not to mention, I stunk like a leaky gas pump.

"I'm fine," I said, looking over my shoulder at Claire and her dad, who were walking up to our little family reunion. "Claire took good care of me."

"No," Claire said, standing next to me. "Luci took good care of *me*." She brushed a hand up to her head.

"We're having a big dinner tonight. For the new year," Abuelita said, speaking English with a heavy accent. "Would you like to stay?" she offered to Claire and Mr. Jacobs.

I had almost forgotten it was New Year's Eve.

"Thank you for such a kind invitation, ma'am," Mr. Jacobs said. "But we have to get going."

"My dad wants to make sure I don't need stitches. He's taking me to the hospital to get me checked out," Claire said with a frown.

My mom nodded. "I think that's a good idea. And tomorrow, we will take Luci to the doctor so she can look at her arm."

"I'm going to miss you so much, Luci," Claire said.

We hugged one more time because somehow through our ordeal in the desert, we had become friends. Real and actual friends.

CHAPTER 17

BIG IDEA

We watched Claire and Mr. Jacobs drive away. When I turned back around to my parents, I caught sight of the cottage and my heart stopped. There was yellow caution tape ribboned around Abuelita's house and X'ed across the front gate.

"Abuelita?" I said.

"It cannot be fixed," she answered, speaking Spanish again.

"No," I whispered. Her pretty rosebush in the front yard had been flattened, probably from inspectors and workers looking at the damage to the house, I guessed. "What are you going to do?" I asked.

"It is an old house," Abuelita said, her eyes full of tears. "Aunt Lorena will host our New Year's Eve party tonight. And I will stay there until I find a new place."

A new place. Would it have a back patio or a garden?

Would there be a park across the street? Would there be room for a wall of framed pictures?

By the time we got to Aunt Lorena's house, it was already full of aunts and uncles and cousins hard at work in the kitchen, preparing for our New Year's Eve feast. Mica ran to Izzy when we walked in and they toddled to the playroom together.

Aunt Lorena came up to me, carrying a towel. "Would you like a bath?" she asked.

"And maybe I should throw out these clothes?" I said with a laugh.

She nodded in agreement. "Your suitcase is in Julieta's room, where you'll be staying for the rest of your trip. Your parents will stay in the guest room. Is that okay?"

I nodded. "Thank you," I said.

I went to Julieta's room and searched my suitcase for some clean clothes. I wanted to wear something special tonight, not only because it was New Year's Eve, but also to celebrate that I was in Chile with my entire family—not to mention that I had just survived a pretty serious ordeal. I pulled out my black sparkly dress that looked like the night sky, and then I took a long, hot shower. I had to soap up twice just to get all the fuel and desert smell off of me.

After I got dressed, I wrapped my hair in a towel and headed back to Julieta's room to get my brush. To my surprise, I found Julieta sitting at her desk.

"Oh!" she said, startled.

"I'm sorry," I said. "Your mom told me to use your room—"

"It's okay," she said, getting up. "I'll go."

"No, don't leave," I said, grabbing my brush from my bag. "Stay. I'll use the bathroom." But then I noticed she had a bunch of mechanical parts scattered on her desk. "What are you working on?"

"I'm putting an old camera back together," Julieta told me.

"That's so cool," I said, realizing the big part at the far end of her desk was a lens. "Hey, congratulations on winning that photography award."

"Thanks." She smiled, looking over her shoulder to some frames hanging on the wall. "I like taking pictures of nature. The beach, animals, flowers . . ."

"Wow, you took these?" I asked, looking at the beautiful pictures: colorful shells, a deer walking across a meadow, a close-up shot of a sunflower. "They're so professional."

She blushed and shrugged. "Maybe not as interesting as being an astronaut."

The old me would have launched into a story about hanging out in the Mars habitat or taking samples in the desert with the NASA scientists, but now nothing was more important than listening to Julieta and learning more about my family.

"Are you kidding?" I said. "I would do anything to learn how to take pictures like this. I'm always amazed when a photo makes me see things differently. How did you take this one?" I asked, pointing to the sunflower photo.

As she described her process, I listened carefully, only speaking up to ask more questions. And before I knew it, we were in a deep conversation about how she used photography to explore strange places. That led us into a conversation about the strange landscape of the Atacama Desert. But this time, when I told her about my experience, she seemed genuinely interested.

I didn't realize how much time had passed until Aunt Lorena called up to Julieta's room to ask if we would go find the other cousins to help set the table.

"They're in the park," Aunt Lorena said, after we rushed down the stairs.

I felt a tingle in my stomach. We were leaving tomorrow and tonight was my last chance to visit with my cousins and try to create some memories with my family. I had to make this time with them count. But would I be able to connect with them like I had with Julieta? Would they give me another chance?

The garage door was open, and I noticed that someone had decorated the trees in the park across the street with twinkly lights. The other three cousins were sitting at a picnic table beneath the lights.

"The park is so beautiful," I said to Julieta, who nodded.

"Hey—" I thought for a second. "I have an idea. What if we set up the party out there, in the park that Abuelita loves so much."

Julieta considered my idea for a moment. "Maybe it would make her feel better to have her New Year's Eve dinner outside," she said.

"It would make for a great family picture too." I nudged her. "And I know a really good photographer."

She poked me back, smiling. "I like this idea. But we're going to need some help. Hugo, Bastian, and Elena!"

My cousins agreed that we would surprise the rest of the family with a New Year's Eve picnic under the stars. We pulled a bunch of picnic tables together to make one giant table under the biggest tree in the park. Then Elena, Julieta, and I ran back to the garage for the tablecloths.

"Hey," I said, skidding to a stop in front of a row of boxes labeled "Abuelita." "Are these from Abuelita's house?"

Julieta nodded, frowning. "They already started packing up the cottage. We are going to store her things here until she finds a new place."

I strode over to one of the boxes, lifted the lid, and looked inside. It was full of picture frames wrapped in newspaper and paper towels. I flipped open the next one: special occasion china. And the next one: trinkets.

"Guys," I said, looking up. "We could use Abuelita's things to set the table. Her dishes are here and we can decorate the table with her favorite memories. She'll be so surprised."

Elena and Julieta looked at each other. "*¡Estupendo!*" Elena said.

They helped me pick out Abuelita's favorite trinkets and framed pictures and load them into a garden wagon.

For a second, I felt a wave of regret that Papa's little toy car wouldn't be there. But I reminded myself that just because the car was gone didn't mean its memory had disappeared.

"This one!" Elena pulled out a rooster saltshaker that was missing its beak. "Remember?" She giggled.

I knew this saltshaker's story: Abuelita's mother got it for Christmas from a neighbor and dropped the package, cracking the shaker before she even had a chance to unwrap it. But instead of jumping in and telling the story myself, I listened to Elena's version.

"We should put the rooster at Abuelita's spot," I said, and we all agreed.

When we had piled the wagon high, we pulled Abuelita's treasures across the park where Hugo and Bastian had just dragged one of Aunt Lorena's good dining room chairs, placing it at the head of the long picnic table for Abuelita. We tossed them the tablecloths and they smoothed the linen across the tables.

"How was your campout the other night?" I asked, carefully taking one of Abuelita's fancy dishes from the wagon and finding a place for it on the table.

"It was fine until *la serpiente*," Julieta said, laughing and giving Bastian a little push.

"A snake?" I said, setting down two more plates. "I really don't like snakes! I would have been terrified!"

"I don't either," Bastian said, his face reddening.

"But it was just a stick!" Hugo clapped his hands, howling.

As we continued setting up, they told me about how one of their friends took such a long time toasting his marshmallow just right, and when it was ready, he dropped it in the fire. I listened, laughing along even though I hadn't been at the campout and I didn't know most of the kids in their stories. But I never once felt left out. In fact, for the first time, I felt like I was really part of their group. So by the time they asked me about my adventures at the habitat, I didn't feel the need to brag or impress them. I told them a shortened version of the story—a story that ended with my favorite part: coming home to my family.

When we were finished decorating the table, we stood back and admired our work. The tablecloths didn't match, most of the plates were chipped, and there were random knickknacks and picture frames scattered about. To a passerby, the table might have looked like a disaster, but to us, it looked just right.

"Luci?" my mom called from Aunt Lorena's driveway. "Luciana?"

"I'll tell them we're ready," I said to my cousins, and they rushed around the table to find their seats on the picnic benches.

When I jogged up to Mom, I could see by the pinched look on her face that she wasn't happy. "Luciana Vega, Aunt Lorena is wondering why her table is not set when dinner is just about out of the oven—"

I stepped aside and motioned to the park. "We thought we'd bring the party to the park. To make Abuelita feel better."

Mom looked at the park and gasped. "It's beautiful. Wait until everyone sees! You did all of this?"

I nodded. "Los Cuatro and I did it together."

She smiled at me, that knowing kind of smile. "I knew you five would come together."

I grinned. "Just tell everyone to come out, okay?"

Soon the entire family was marching across the park, their arms full of bowls and pitchers and platters. When she saw the table, Abuelita let out a little shriek of happiness.

I held out the chair for her at the head of the table. "You're our special guest, Abuelita," I said.

She sat down. "Oh, *mi gallo*!" she said, patting the rooster at her plate. "This is so wonderful!" She inspected the trinkets and pictures, and looked at the lights in the tree above us that twinkled like stars. "Gracias, Luci."

"It was all of us," I said, motioning to the rest of the cousins.

"I should have known," Abuelita said. *"Los Cinco."* The Five.

I looked over at my cousins, and they gave me a huge smile.

"Los Cinco," Julieta said. "I like that."

As everyone took their seats, the aunts and uncles began passing around the food and drinks from Aunt Lorena's house. There was ensalada a la chilena, beef *empanadas*, and fresh corn cakes steamed in corn husks. We all made sure to serve ourselves extra grapes and boiled lentils for good luck in the new year, a Chilean tradition.

But then I caught a glimpse of the cottage behind my family, dark and shuttered, and I looked at Abuelita.

"I'm sorry you can't take all of your things with you to Aunt Lorena's house. And—" I stopped, swallowing, afraid to tell her about Papa's toy car. "Also, I'm sorry because I lost Papa's car in the earthquake. I never should have brought it with me."

Abuelita put her fork down. "Niña, do not be sorry. You are here and safe and that's all that matters. Even though the car is gone, we can still hold on to the story."

I nodded, and held her hand. "Maybe we can hold on to the memories from your house the same way," I said. "In our hearts."

Abuelita sighed, sitting back in her chair and smiling. Also crying. But mostly smiling. "Yes," she said, wiping her eyes, and looking over to her shuttered cottage. "I think you're right. That is a good reminder."

I scooted closer to her to give her a hug.

Soon the littlest cousins were squawking to leave the table and go to the playground, and the aunts and uncles started stacking plates to take back to the kitchen. Abuelita rubbed my good shoulder, smiling. "I don't want this night to end. Thank you, Luciana."

And then I remembered, standing up fast in my seat. "Wait!"

Everyone froze.

"We have one more thing to do," I said, looking at Julieta, who grabbed her camera. "A photo," I said to Abuelita. "For when you start a new wall of family pictures in your new home."

Abuelita clapped and together, my cousins and I helped gather everyone in front of the tree with all the lights for a New Year's Eve picture. Julieta set up the camera with an automatic timer, and I was pretty sure my eyes were closed and there was a good chance Izzy was pulling Dad's hair, but I didn't care. It was a picture of all of us together, squished in tight so every aunt, uncle, and cousin was in the frame.

Nobody was left out.

Mission accomplished.

GLOSSARY

adiós (*ah-dee-OHS*) good-bye

asado (*ah-SAH-do*) barbecue

bienvenidas (*bee-en-veh-NEE-dahs*) welcome (plural
  feminine)

Buenos días, mi amor. (*BWEH-nohs DEE-ahs mee
  ah-MOR*) Good morning, my love.

cabeza (*kah-BAY-sah*) head

Chilena (*chee-LAY-nah*) Chilean (feminine)

choripanes (*cho-ree-PAHN-es*) Chilean sandwiches
  made with sausage and crusty bread

¿Comiste? (*ko-MEES-tay*) Did you eat?

¿Cómo estuvo el viaje? (*KO-mo es-TOO-vo el vee-
  AH-hay*) How was the trip?

corazón (*cor-a-SOHN*) heart

empanadas (*em-pah-NAH-dahs*) a pastry or bread stuffed with sweet or savory filling

ensalada a la chilena (*en-sah-LAH-dah a la chee-LAY-nah*) Chilean salad

Está bien (*es-TAH bee-EN*) It's okay

¿Estás cansada? (*es-TAHS cahn-SAH-dah*) Are you tired?

¿Están heridos? (*es-TAHN air-EE-dohs*) Are you injured? (plural)

¡Estupendo! (*es-too-PEN-doh*) Fabulous!

gracias (*GRAH-see-ahs*) thank you

hola (*OH-la*) hi

la serpiente (*la sayr-pee-EN-tay*) the snake

lo siento (*lo see-EN-toh*) I'm sorry

Los Cinco (*los SEEN-ko*) The Five

Los Cuatro (*los CWA-tro*) The Four

mi gallo (*mee GAH-yo*) my rooster

mi niña (*mee NEEN-yah*) my girl

¡Mis niñas grandes! (*mees NEEN-yahs GRAHN-des*) My big girls!

muy fuertes (*moo-ee FWER-tehs*) very strong

Necesitamos el azúcar. (*neh-seh-see-TAH-mos el ah-SOO-kar*) We need the sugar.

pan de Pascua (*pahn day PAHS-kwah*) a Chilean cake
  traditionally eaten at Christmas time
parrilla (*pah-REE-yah*) grill / barbecue
pebre (*PEH-bray*) a Chilean condiment
sí (*see*) yes
temblor (*tem-BLOR*) tremor
terremoto (*teh-reh-MO-toh*) earthquake
¡Un momento! (*oon mo-MEN-toh*) One moment!

ABOUT THE AUTHOR

Erin Teagan is the author of *The Friendship Experiment* and worked in science for more than ten years before becoming a writer. She uses many of her experiences from the lab in her books and loves sharing the best and most interesting (and most dangerous and disgusting) parts of science with kids. Erin lives in Virginia with her family, a puppy named Beaker, and a bunny that thinks he's a cat. Visit her at www.erinteagan.com.

AUTHOR'S NOTE

In *Luciana: Out of This World*, Luciana spends time on the Mars Habitat in the Atacama Desert in northern Chile. The Atacama Desert is one of the driest and most barren deserts in the world, experiencing little to no rain each year. Its clear skies make it a hub for astronomical studies and the desert is home to many important telescopes. Scientists have compared the extreme dryness of the Atacama Desert to the harsh environment on Mars. This makes the desert an ideal setting for NASA to test equipment, such as rovers, space suits, and chemistry kits for testing soil, that may be used on Mars one day. Although *Luciana: Out of this World* is fictional, and NASA would not typically allow kids to participate in these missions, Luciana's story was inspired by real work scientists are doing in the Atacama Desert.

SPECIAL THANKS

With gratitude to astronaut Dr. Megan McArthur; Dr. Ellen Stofan, former chief scientist at NASA; Maureen O'Brien, manager of strategic alliances at NASA; Dr. Brian Glass, principal investigator of the Atacama Rover Astrobiology Drilling Studies project at NASA; Dr. Mary Beth Wilhelm, NASA Astrobiologist; Lisa Spence, NASA Flight Analogs Project Manager; Mallory Jennings, NASA Spacesuit Engineer; and the rest of the NASA Headquarters and Johnson Space Center teams, for their insights and knowledge of space exploration.

REACH
FOR THE STARS
WITH
Luciana

VISIT
americangirl.com to learn more about
Luciana's world!

Parents, request a FREE catalogue at
americangirl.com/catalogue

Sign up at **americangirl.com/email**
to receive the latest news and exclusive offers

Meet Gabriela McBride™

When the city threatens to close her beloved community arts center, Gabriela is determined to find a way to help. Can she harness the power of her words and rally her community to save Liberty Arts?

Meet TENNEY Grant™

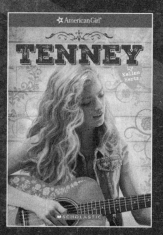

Her biggest dream is to share what's in her heart through music. Little does she know, she's about to get the opportunity of a lifetime.

A group of girls so close, they're just

Like Sisters

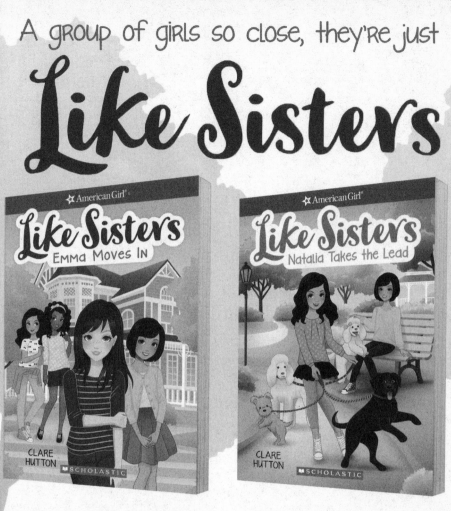

Emma loves visiting her twin cousins, Natalia and Zoe, so she's thrilled when her family moves to their town after living 3,000 miles away. Emma knows her life is about to change in a big way. And it will be more wonderful and challenging than any of the girls expect!

There's going to be a wedding at the inn—with dog ring bearers! Natalia loves dogs and offers to watch and walk them. But has Natalia bitten off more than she can chew? When one of the dogs goes missing, Natalia enlists Emma, Caitlin, and Zoe to help. If they can't find the dog, the wedding will be wrecked!

Explore real historical events with the American Girls!

In 1773, revolution was in the air in Boston! Read about the famous protest that pushed the rebellious American colonies and the British closer to war.

This "unsinkable" ship turned out to be very sinkable. Learn what it was like to be on the infamous ship when it sank in arctic waters in 1912.

Secrets, disguises, and courageous escapes—read about real slaves' journeys to freedom on the Underground Railroad.